Pippa's P

There is no such thing as the Pippa Jinx!

The point is that if a person has a whole heap of ideas, then you've got to expect a few of them to go wrong sometimes. But, like my mom says, the important thing is to *learn* from mistakes. Sure, my mom also said that the number of mistakes I'd already made probably meant I'd learned more in my first ten years than most people did in a whole lifetime, but that didn't mean I should just *give up*. It simply meant I needed to think really carefully before I came up with advice for Barbra. So . . . I did just that!

Check out some of the other great books
in the Stacy and Friends series

1. The Great Sister War
2. Pippa's Problem Page
3. My Sister, My Slave
4. My Real Best Friend

Pippa's Problem Page

Allan Frewin Jones

Series created by Ben M. Baglio

RED FOX

A Red Fox Book

Published by Random House Children's Books
20 Vauxhall Bridge Road, London SW1V 2SA

A division of Random House UK Ltd
London Melbourne Sydney Auckland
Johannesburg and agencies throughout the world

1 3 5 7 9 10 8 6 4 2

Printed and bound in Great Britain by
Cox & Wyman Ltd, Reading, Berkshire

Papers used by Random House UK Limited
are natural, recyclable products made from wood grown in sustainable forest. The manufacturing processes conform to the enviromental regulations of the country of origin.

RANDOM HOUSE UK Limited Reg No. 954009

ISBN 0 09 926358 0

Dear Louella Parsnips,

I'm really glad that you started up your problem hotline. I have a real bad problem. I'd just like to point out that it is kind of weird that people have to leave their letters in an unused locker round back of the broken drinks machine in the corridor by the gym. Oh – that isn't my problem, by the way. I just thought I'd mention it. I have a question for you.

Why don't you find a better place for people to leave their letters? A private mail box number, or something?

That isn't *the* question. That's just *a* question. It doesn't have anything to do with the question I wanted to ask or the real bad problem I have right now.

I really hope you can help me with my problem.

I look forward to your prompt reply.

Yours,

Cindy

Dear Louella Parsnips,

Hi! It's me again. Did you get my last letter? I guess you must have done, because I checked the unused locker round back of the broken drinks machine in the corridor by the gym and my letter was gone. If you have already read my last letter you might be able to guess why I went back to the unused locker . . . blah, blah. I suddenly remembered I forgot to tell you what my real big problem is.

I know what you are probably thinking – you are thinking that my real big problem is my *memory*. Well, that is not true. I have a really good memory usually. I guess I just got kind of flustered because I was trying to write the letter in secret so people wouldn't know I had a problem, and my friend Fern dropped a splodge of strawberry yoghurt on my foot and it surprised me and made me forget what I was writing about.

I'm writing this letter in bed first thing in the morning so there isn't anyone around to splodge strawberry yoghurt on my foot. Do you like strawberry yoghurt? I do. But not on my foot.

Anyhow, *my problem*.

The thing is that a few weeks back I asked my folks for a clarinet. I thought it would be really neat to learn to play the clarinet, and maybe get into the school orchestra. My friend Fern says asking for a clarinet was dumb. She says I should have asked for an electric guitar or a synthesiser. But I asked my best friend, Stacy, what musical instrument I should ask for, and she said, 'Ask for a small one, because then it's no big hassle carrying it around.' I thought that was pretty neat advice.

My other pal, Pippa, said I should ask for a drum, because that would be real easy to learn. Like, you just *hit* it, right? But Stacy said that a drum would be a big hassle on the school bus and stuff. She also reminded me that Pippa's advice is always wrong. So, I went for a clarinet because that is only small.

My folks bought me the clarinet. Apparently it was real expensive, so Mom said I had to practise every day or it would be a *big waste of money*. Well, the thing I didn't know was that a clarinet is a totally, utterly and completely impossible musical instrument to play unless you are prepared to spend the whole of your life practising it!!!! It just makes razzing noises all the time and if I blow real hard it makes my ears pop, which I don't think can be right.

Anyway, I told my mom that maybe a

clarinet wasn't such a brilliant musical instrument for me to learn after all, as it made my ears pop and only came out with razzing noises, and could I maybe have a drum instead? And could she make it a real small drum, and not one of those huge timpani kind of things because that would be a total nightmare on the school bus?

Well, Mom was totally uncooperative! Like, she said I'd nagged her ragged about the clarinet (not true! I only mentioned it, like, a couple of times. Well, maybe *three or four* times, but no more often, honest!) and she said that she had gone to a lot of trouble to get one for me, and now I could darned well put a little effort into learning to play it. I tried to explain about my ears and all that stuff, but she just wouldn't listen. (She's like that sometimes – totally unreasonable!)

So, my problem is this: Mom insists I practise on that darned clarinet every single solitary day of the week, except for Saturday and Sunday and Wednesday. Oh, and I'm allowed most Mondays and Fridays off, too. But I'm being forced to practise the stupid thing every *other* day of the week and it's driving me crazy. One day my ears are going to go pop *permanently* and I won't be able to hear any more. I'm sure of it! I have told my mom about this, but she just won't listen. It will serve her right if I go deaf.

Help! Help! Help! How can I get out of practising the clarinet without my mom going postal on me?

A quick reply would be appreciated.

Yours,

Cindy

PS Don't bother suggesting I fake a burglary in which the clarinet is stolen. I tried that one and Mom didn't believe me. She turned my room upside down until she found the clarinet under my mattress. I told her I must have put it there in my sleep. I think I convinced her, but she sure won't go for the burglary scam *twice*.

Put your very best thinking cap on, Louella!

C.

PPS Please mark your reply envelope 'C'.

Thanks.

C.

Dear Cindy,

I have given your intractorable problem a considerable amount of deep thought. I feel I may have come up with an answer which will relieve you of the undoubted burden of having to practise a musical instrument to which you are neither temperamentally nor physically suited. (I am very concerned about the effect that it is having on your ears. Have you tried wedging half a dozen Q Tips into your ears before you start to blow? I believe this may help.)

There is a girl in 5th Grade who plays clarinet in the school orchestra. Her name is Devon Palminieri. It has come to my attention that Devon is having trouble practising at home because she has seven brothers and three sisters. And she has to share a room with two of her sisters – because there is not enough room in their house for everyone to have their own room – which I think is totally terrible, and I certainly could not cope with sharing *my* room!

My solution to your intractorable problem is that you should speak to Devon and suggest that she should practise her clarinet round your house two or three times a week. Then all you have to do is sneak her into your room without your mom noticing. Your mom will then hear Devon practising the clarinet and she will think it is you. (You will also have to sneak Devon out of your house, don't forget.)

You will not only be saving your ears, but

you will also be helping Devon out a whole lot.

Yours problem-answeringly,

Louella Parsnips

'Pippa! The food's on the table, honey!'

'OK, Mom,' I called. 'Coming!' I folded up my brilliantly thought-out reply letter and slid it into an envelope. I addressed it 'For C.' A lot of my clients like the anonymous touch. I mean, face it, who wants the whole world to know you have problems you can't figure out for yourself, huh? I sure wouldn't.

Hey, and who'd have thought Cindy would need my help?

Oh, I just thought of something. You're probably wondering how come my mom called me 'Pippa' just then when my name is Louella Parsnips. Well, the truth is that Louella Parsnips isn't my real name at all. It's my *professional* name. My real name is Pippa Kane.

And I'm not a full-time advice columnist or problem-solver either. A person really would think I did it for a living the way I write my replies, though. I take a whole lot of trouble to make them look totally professional. That's why I put in unusual-type words like 'intractorable'. It means really, really difficult. Impressive, huh? The fact is, I know a whole heap of words like that. My mom is a college professor. My dad is really smart, too, but he's busy being really smart over the other side of the country. Yeah, my folks split up. Total misery! I was really torn up about it at the time, but I've gotten *almost* used to it by now. Like Mom says, life has to go on. Even when it means that Dad is in New Mexico and Mom and I are stuck here in Four Corners, Indiana.

I say 'stuck' – but it's not like that really. I like our town a lot and I have some great friends here. You'll meet up with them as we go along. Well, you've already met Cindy Spiegel – kind of. She wrote the 'clarinet' letter. Both letters, in fact! You might think from reading her first letter, that Cindy is a little slow, you know? But she isn't really – Fern can be *very* distracting, and I guess having someone dollop strawberry yoghurt on your foot would be enough to put anyone off.

Fern is Fern Kipsak. She's small and loud and messy and she wears strange clothes which I think her folks get from a special 'Strange Clothes R Us' store somewhere. She has long straight brown hair with a centre parting. I guess you might call her a slacker, but she says she's a hippy. Don't ask! Still, I really like Fern. I guess, if I had to choose, I'd say she's my best friend although we're totally different people. (Maybe she's my best friend *because* we're totally different people?)

Cindy's best friend is Stacy Allen. That's the whole gang – me and Fern and Stacy and Cindy. We call it a 'gang' but I prefer to think of it as a select *club*. My mom told me about a club that used to meet years ago in New York. It was called the Algonquin Club. It was full of intellectuals and journalists and really smart and interesting people. They'd meet up regularly and have these really wonderful, witty conversations.

I tried to get the guys to agree to calling our gang the 'Pippagonquin Club', but they said it was a dumb, stupid, useless name which no one would ever remember. We spent a whole lot of time trying to come up with a real neat name for our club. Cindy suggested the Mitten Club. Gaaah! Cindy, I have to warn you, can be a little *nerdy* at times. She said it would be a great name because we all fitted together like hands do in mittens. I mean, *really*! I ask you!

Mind you, Fern suggested the 'Close Encounters Club'. I took her to one side and asked: *why?* Well, you *would*, wouldn't you? Anyhow, she said, 'Because Four Corners is full of aliens.'

And I said, 'What aliens? I've never seen any aliens.'

And Fern said, 'Of course not – they're *hiding*!'

Fern is kind of crazy and confused if you ask me, but she makes me laugh!

Stacy's idea for a gang name was the 'Allen Clan'. That idea only got one vote.

Anyhow, we never did agree on a gang name. It's like that sometimes with us. I still think the Pippagonquin Club would have been mega neat!

I'm sorry, I got carried away there a little – I was meaning to tell you how come I became Louella Parsnips, brilliant, mysterious, undercover problem-solver to Four Corners Middle School.

Well, it's a real good story, I think. And it all started that day when the new girl arrived in our class.

Important Correction:

You know I told you how I like to use unusual words in my replies as Louella Parsnips, Problem-Solver to Four Corners Middle School? Well, I've just found out that there's no such word as 'intractorable'. Rats!

How did I find out? Well, I had this tricky piece of math homework, and I said to my mom: 'This problem is kind of intractorable, Mom. Could you help out?'

She *did* help out – but not before she spent, like, three hours rolling around the house clutching at her sides and yelling with laughter.

Apparently the word is 'intractable'.

I prefer 'intractorable' myself. And, hey, who makes these words up in the first place, huh? I don't see why I can't use 'intractorable' if I feel like it. Maybe if I use it often enough it'll catch on and everyone will start using it, and then maybe it'll wind up in a dictionary in a few years' time.

Who'll have the last laugh, then? Me, that's who!

Barbra Plum turned up in our class one Monday morning in the middle of term. Ms Fenwick, our homeroom teacher, introduced her to us and told us that she'd be with us for a couple of months. Ms Fenwick told us that Barbra's mom was working temporarily in Four Corners on secondment – whatever that is.

Barbra looked like an OK kind of person. She had a friendly, freckly face and long straight black hair. I have long boring straight black hair, too, so I could sympathise with her about that! I keep my long boring straight black hair in a thick braid down my back. I'd really like to have curly auburn hair like Cindy. Cindy says she'd like straight hair like mine. Fern says she'd like to shave her head and have 'Wild Thing' tattooed across her scalp, but her folks won't let her. I can see their point.

Stacy has freckles and she hates them. I wouldn't mind freckles. Is no one in the entire world happy with how they look?

Anyway, back to Barbra. The way things work in our school is that if a new person arrives in the middle of the year, they're allocated a 'pal' to show them the ropes and help them get used to how things run.

Barbra got me.

I was really pleased, because looking after a newcomer is a real responsibility, and Betsy-Jane Garside would have just *loved* to have taken Barbra under her wing. Betsy-Jane thinks she's real smart, but she's just a total show-off, if you ask me. Barbra was going to be a whole lot better off under my guidance. And she'd learn who were *good people* and who were *show-offs* and who were people *best avoided*. Put me and Fern and Cindy and Stacy in the first category; Betsy-Jane in the second, and people like Judy MacWilliams in 8th Grade in the last one. Definitely!

Anyway, in morning break we found out some stuff about Barbra. Her folks had split up a few months back and she was here in Four Corners with her mom. They came originally from Salt Lake City. This was like a kind of extended stopover, and in a couple of months they would be moving on to Atlantic City. Like Fern said, some folks sure do get around!

Barbra seemed kind of quiet, but then I guess *anyone* would seem quiet next to Fern. It took a couple of days, but Barbra finally opened up to me a little one morning when we were on our own, walking between classes.

'Pippa,' she said, 'does your mom embarrass you at all?'

I thought about this.

'She laughs her head off if I get words wrong,' I said. I looked at her. 'Is that the kind of thing you mean?'

'Uh . . . no, not really.' Barbra shook her head. She gave me an anxious look. 'Does she . . . uh . . . does she *dance* with the shopping trolley in the supermarket?'

'Excuse me?'

'My mom does these little dances up and down the aisles . . . with the shopping trolley,' Barbra explained. 'And she sings.' Barbra looked around to make sure no one was watching, then she did a little zigzag jig along the corridor with her hands out like someone steering a trolley, and she went: 'La di dah, dee-doo dee-dum, dee-doo dee-dee . . .'

She looked glumly at me. 'She is always doing stuff like that. She says it makes shopping fun. It embarrasses the heck out of me, but if I say anything, she just laughs and tells me to loosen up.' Barbra gave me a horrified look. 'What can you do with a mom like that?'

I blinked at her.

'And that's not all,' Barbra said. 'Every morning when she drops me off at school she . . .' Barbra shuddered, '. . . she gives me a big red lipsticky kiss.' She pointed to her forehead. 'Right there. Like I'm some kind of total infant. And her lipstick comes off on me. And I have to walk all the way to the bathroom before I can be sure I've wiped it all off. And *look* at what she makes me *wear*!' She tugged at her chunky knitted sweater. 'I mean – just *look* at it!'

I looked at it.

I'm really too polite to make comments about people's choice of clothes. I mean, if your best pal walks around like an explosion in a psychedelic garment factory, you get kind of used to the fact that people sometimes have eccentric taste in clothes. Take for instance the sweater that Barbra was wearing right then. It was beastly blue around the top and gruesome green around the bottom and it had yucky yellow knitted rabbits hopping all around it.

Score for nerdishness: ten out of ten with *honours*.

Score for cool and street-cred: a big fat *zero*.

'I . . . see . . .' I said.

'It's a nightmare,' Barbra said.

'Yes. I see.'

'A total nightmare!' Barbra looked appealingly at me. 'I have a totally nightmare mom.

You have to help me, Pippa. What should I *do*?'

I smiled reassuringly at her. 'Leave it with me, Barbra,' I said. 'I'll give it some thought and then I'll get back to you, OK?'

Barbra gave me this totally relieved look. 'Really?' she said. 'You can help?'

'Sure,' I said. 'No problem.'

Well, when you're asked to be a new person's 'pal', the least you can do is iron out a few bugs for her, huh?

'Guess what, guys,' I said, later that afternoon. Our gang was all together in Fern's bedroom after school. 'Barbra has some problems, and she's asked me to help her out with them.'

'You?' Fern shrieked with laughter. 'YOU?'

'Yes,' I said in a real dignified way. 'Why not?'

Cindy was grinning like an idiot. 'Pippa, you're one of my all-time best friends and all that, but you're the last person in the entire world I'd ask for *advice*.'

'Well, thanks!'

'Pippa,' Stacy laughed, 'you're totally *jinxed*! You know you are.'

'I don't know any such thing!' I retorted. *Really*, those guys, sometimes!

'What about that time Cindy's pillow caught fire?' Fern said. 'And the fire brigade turned up and –'

I glared at her. 'I thought we'd agreed never to mention that again,' I said.

I mean, it was the kind of thing that could happen to *anyone*. Cindy had been writing her secret diary in bed and her red pen had leaked all over her pillowcase. And when she'd taken the pillowcase off, the ink had gotten all over her pillow, too.

The problem was that her mom had only just finished giving her a lecture about not writing her secret diary in bed because of getting pen-marks on the sheets, so she needed to clear up the mess without her mom finding out. So, like anyone would, she came to her friends for advice.

I had a brilliant idea. She could wash the pillow in the machine and dry it in the drier, and the whole thing would be done and dusted before her mom knew a single thing about it. And it all went fine until the stupid pillow decided to burst open in the drier. Somehow the feathers got into the works and all this smelly smoke started billowing out.

Well, the next thing she knew, there were firemen all over and her mom came home from work to find the whole house stinking like nothing on earth and the tumble drier full of blackened, smoking feathers.

And, of course, *I* got the blame!

'And what about that time you were helping Stacy to hang that picture in her bedroom and you picked a spot on the wall that meant she hammered a nail right through a water pipe?' said Cindy. She grinned around at the others. 'Remember that?' Fern grinned. I noticed that Stacy didn't grin all that much. I guess she still remembered the way the jet of water squirted clear across the room and nearly *skwooshalised* her cat, Benjamin, right out the window.

'And what about that time when Fern was saving the labels off food cans for a competition to win a vacation in Hawaii?' Stacy said. 'And you suggested she take the labels off a whole heap of cans in advance and then no one knew what was in any of the cans and Fern didn't know if she was gonna have stewed prunes or baked beans or tinned soup for dinner for two weeks!'

'*And* I didn't even win the competition,' Fern reminded everyone. 'Because you – ' meaning me – 'said that it was good luck to let someone else mail the letter and you put the envelope with the company's address on inside the reply envelope with my address on it, and the letter came back to me and I missed the deadline.'

'Have you guys *finished*?' I yelled. 'I don't see what any of that stuff has to do with the fact that Barbra Plum has asked me for some advice.'

'Face it, Pippa,' Fern said. 'The only way your advice could come in useful is if a person does the exact *opposite* of what you tell 'em. Trust me.'

'On the other hand,' said Stacy, 'if you tell us what Barbra's problem is, we might be able to help her out.'

Cindy giggled. 'So long as *you* don't say a *word*,' she said to me.

I stood up. 'Well,' I said crossly, 'if you're through making fun of me, I think I'll just go home now.' I marched to the door. 'And I think I'll keep Barbra's problems to myself, thanks,' I said. 'I'll work on them without your help.' I grabbed the door handle and gave it a fierce twist. 'Some people have a little faith in me! *Some* people do!' There was a cracking noise and the handle came off in my hand.

I stared down at that stupid handle. Why did it choose *that* moment to break, huh?

'The Pippa Jinx!' Fern yelled with laughter.

You know, sometimes I get the feeling that the whole world is lined up just waiting to make me look silly.

There is no such thing as the Pippa Jinx!

The point is that if a person has a whole heap of ideas, then you've got to expect a few of them to go wrong sometimes. But, like my mom says, the important thing is to *learn* from mistakes. Sure, my mom also said that the number of mistakes I'd already made probably meant I'd learned more in my first ten years than most people did in a whole lifetime, but that didn't mean I should just *give up*. It simply meant I needed to think really carefully before I came up with advice for Barbra.

So, I did just that!

'Hey! Barbra!'

Barbra looked all around, up and down, and behind her, too.

'Psst! over here!'

At last she spotted me, hiding down the stairs that led to the utility room. It was the next morning and I had come up with some great ideas to solve Barbra's problems. But I had to make sure the other guys weren't around when I told her my great ideas. They might tell her stuff that would destroy her faith in me. That was why I got to school early and hid myself away until Barbra arrived.

Barbra stared down at me over the banister.

'Pippa? What are you doing down there?'

'Shhh!' I beckoned her down.

'Are you OK?' Barbra asked.

'Yes, fine,' I said. 'I've been thinking real hard and I've come up with some ideas about how to deal with your mom.'

Barbra looked at me as if she thought I was a little strange.

'Why do you have to tell me down here?' she whispered.

I blinked at her. 'Uh . . .'

'And why are we whispering?' she whispered.

'Uh . . .'

'Do I have lipstick on my forehead?' she asked.

I nodded and pointed at a red smear just above her left eyebrow. She rubbed at it. I nodded. 'It's gone,' I said. 'Now, do you want to hear my ideas or not?'

'I sure do,' Barbra said with a big sigh. 'It's supermarket day today.'

'OK, here goes –'

My ideas were fiendish in their simplicity, even though I say so myself. I've found in the past that the more complicated you make things, the more likely they are to go wrong. These were sure-fire, can't-possibly-go-wrong kind of ideas.

The Supermarket Dilemma

Suggest to your mom that the whole miserable business of food shopping could be speeded up if you took *two* trolleys into the supermarket and each had half the shopping list. Suggest that you split up, pick up all the stuff on your half-lists, then meet up at the checkout. *Voilà!* (That's French for Yo! Problem solved!) You get around the supermarket in half the time, your mom thinks you're wonderful for being so helpful, and the best part of it is that she can dance with the trolley all she likes and sing her head off, and no one will know she has anything to do with you. (Extra idea: you could even say stuff to people like, 'Gee, I'm really glad I don't know that crazy woman doing the dancing and the singing over there!')

The Terrible Kissing Thing

You have to realise right from the start that it's totally impossible to stop your mom from kissing you if she's determined to do it.

A couple of ideas I rejected:

1. Wear a paper bag over your head.

Excellent protection but too obvious. This will leave you open to questions such as: 'Why are you wearing a paper bag over your head?' Mom will probably say: 'Take that stupid paper bag off.' Removal of the paper bag will result in the Terrible Kissing Thing.

2. Smear your forehead with something that tastes awful.

Preferred outcome: Mom will kiss you as usual. She will taste the awful thing you have smeared on your forehead. She will go '*Yuck*!' After a couple of days of this she will give up kissing you. This is known as *aversion therapy*.

Likely outcome: Mom will want to know why you have mustard/vinegar/furniture polish/lime juice/dishwashing liquid/wasp repellent/etc on your forehead. She will make you wipe it off. She may think you've gone insane and she may arrange for you to see a child psychiatrist. The Terrible Kissing Thing will happen twice as much as before because she will be worried about why you are smearing mustard/vinegar . . . etc on your forehead.

As you can see, I'd given Barbra's problem a lot of thought. The solution I'd come up with was F in its S (Fiendish in its Simplicity – see above).

If you can't stop her kissing you, then at least you can reduce the fallout by hiding her lipstick! No big embarrassing red smear to worry about!

Barbra thought about these ideas for a while.

'Of course,' I said, 'you could always just *ask* her to stop dancing and singing in the supermarket.' Barbra stared blankly at me. 'Uh, and you could always just ask her not to kiss you when she drops you off at school.'

Barbra shook her head. 'You don't know my mom,' she said in a really dismal voice. 'If I asked her to stop she'd do it twice as much.' She sighed. 'I think she just likes to embarrass me.'

'Parents can be a total pain,' I said sympathetically. I could understand how Barbra must feel, even though my own mom isn't really all that bad. The only truly horrifying thing my mom does is when she balances on the couch in our living room and pretends to conduct the orchestra when she's listening to her classical music CDs. And at least that only happens behind closed doors!

Barbra had a good long think about my ideas. 'Yes,' she said, at last, 'I'll try it out.' She smiled. 'Thanks, Pippa. You might have saved my life!'

'Uh, one thing,' I said. 'I think it might be best if we don't talk about this in front of other people. Uh, people like . . . Fern, and, uh . . . Stacy. People like that.'

'Why not?'

'Excuse me?'

'Why shouldn't we talk about these things in front of Fern and Stacy?'

'I didn't mean *just* Fern and Stacy,' I said quickly. 'They were just an example. I meant, uh, people in general, you know?'

'Why not?'

I frowned. 'Because it's unlucky,' I said with sudden inspiration. 'Yeah, that's it. I don't know what it's like where you come from, but in Four Corners, it's considered real unlucky to talk about good ideas in front of people.' I nodded encouragingly. 'Talking about good ideas means they get jinxed. Honest.'

'OK,' Barbra said with a smile. 'If you say so.'

Phew! Trying to give people good advice can be real difficult when you have friends like mine. I mean, face it, if Fern and the bunch knew I was giving Barbra advice, they'd tell her a whole heap of horror stories about me.

And knowing Fern and Stacy and Cindy they'd *exaggerate* like crazy, and wind up making me look . . . well . . . *jinxed*!

And, like I said, there's no such thing as the Pippa Jinx!

I guess you're expecting me to tell you that everything went haywire when Barbra tried out my ideas on her mom.

Totally wrong!

I was in homeroom at school the following morning, waiting with everyone else for Ms Fenwick to arrive and register us, when Barbra came running in grinning like a Cheshire Cat who has tickly underwear and who's just heard a really funny joke.

'Pippa! It was brilliant!' she said as she came crashing up to my desk. 'It all worked totally *perfectly*!'

'What did?' Fern asked. She sits next to me in homeroom. Stacy and Cindy sit in front of us. They looked around, too.

'Oh, nothing much,' I said casually. 'I gave Barbra some advice about some problems she was having with her mom, that's all.'

'Uh-oh!' said Stacy. She looked at Barbra. 'You didn't actually do anything Pippa suggested, did you?'

'I sure did!' Barbra said.

Fern shook her head. 'Ba-ad move!' she said. 'Mega-bad move, Barbra.'

'Not at all!' Barbra said. 'It all went perfectly.'

'So, what did she tell you to do?' asked Cindy.

Barbra explained my idea about the shopping trolleys. 'And Mom thought it was a really great idea,' she said. 'She said we should shop like that from now on.' Her eyes lit up. 'And I hid her lipstick in her underwear drawer this morning,' she said, 'and she didn't have time to look for it.' She pointed to her forehead. 'No lipsticky kissy-mark!' She smiled at me. 'Pippa, you're a total genius, I'm telling you! You ought to . . . to . . . you ought to write an advice column for a magazine! That's what you ought to do!'

This was greeted by my so-called friends by yells and splutters of laughter.

I looked at Barbra. '*Now* do you see why I didn't want certain *people* to know I was helping you out?' I said. I glared at my friends. 'Certain people seem to think I never give good advice. Certain people think that everything I say is, like, totally *stupid*.' I had to raise my voice, they were laughing so much. 'Certain people wouldn't know good advice if it came up and bit them on the bottom!'

'OK, everyone, settle down now!' Ms Fenwick had arrived.

'I'll catch you later,' Barbra said as she scuttled over to her own desk.

'You see?' I hissed at three laughing hyenas called Stacy, Fern and Cindy. 'Some people appreciate me!'

'She'll learn,' said Fern. 'She'll learn when the Pippa Jinx hits!'

I snorted in irritation, but I didn't say anything.

Miss Fenwick pulled out the register book and began to call our names out.

I'd *proved* I could give good advice, but my so-called best friends still thought I was a total *hoodoo*! It was darned *annoying*! Something had to be done to convince them that I wasn't disaster-prone!

But what?

We were in the cafeteria at lunchtime. The four of us have a favourite table in a corner where we always eat, but as a special concession we'd pulled up another chair for Barbra. (We're usually pretty fussy about who we allow to sit with us, but we'd decided that Barbra was a unique case.)

Stacy was complaining about her thirteen-year-old sister, Amanda. Stacy's sister is this big blonde air-head bimbo. I sure wouldn't want her as *my* sister. Right then, Stacy's beef was that Amanda was always hogging the phone.

'She acts like she owns the thing,' Stacy said.

‘Every time I want to call anyone, she’s there first, blabbing to one of her dimwit friends.’ Stacy glared darkly over to a table on the other side of the room, where Amanda and her dimwit friends were doubtlessly having one of their endless dimwit conversations about absolutely nothing at all.

‘Maybe you could suggest she has her own line?’ Barbra said.

‘I tried that,’ Stacy moaned. ‘Mom said the phone bills are high enough without Amanda having a line all to herself.’ Stacy sighed. ‘And Dad said it would be *cruel* to allow her twenty-four-hour access to a phone, ’cos she’d wear her jaw out with all the yakking.’

‘I have an idea,’ I said.

‘Have you thought of superglue chewing gum?’ Fern said. ‘Spread superglue on a stick of gum and give it to Amanda. She won’t be able to spend all day on the phone with her teeth glued together.’

‘I have an idea, guys,’ I said a little louder.

‘Maybe you could hide the phone?’ Cindy said.

‘Or make a whole bunch of crank calls!’ Fern suggested. ‘You could use different voices.’ She put on a deep, gravelly voice. ‘Hello? Is that Amanda Allen? I just called to tell you that you smell like old socks!’ She laughed. ‘Then you hang up. Wait until she gets back to her room, then call again.' This time Fern's voice was high-pitched and squeaky. 'Amanda Allen? Did you know a state-wide poll has just confirmed that you have the brains of a lima bean?'

'I have a really good idea, you guys,' I said even louder.

'What is it?' Barbra asked.

'I'm very glad you asked, Barbra,' I said to her. 'As everyone else around here seems to be ignoring me, I'll tell you. I think Stacy and Amanda should plan out a schedule for using the phone. Like, Amanda could use the phone between 7.30 and 8.00 in the morning. Then Stacy could use it between 8.00 and 8.30. And so on through the day. Both of them would sign the agreement and promise to stick to it, or face a forfeit – like, doing the other person's chores for a day, or something.'

'That sounds OK,' Barbra said.

'Exactly!' I said.

'It wouldn't work,' Fern said.

'Oh yeah?' I asked. 'And why not?'

'One simple reason,' Fern said. She pointed to me. '*You* thought of it.'

Arrrgh!

That did it! *Things had got to change around here*!

The very next morning a strange and mysterious advertisement was found pinned to the notice board in the corridor where our lockers are kept.

FREE ADVICE!!!!!!!
UNIQUE OFFER!!!!
A NOT-TO-BE-MISSED OPPORTUNITY!
Do you have worries? Problems? Concerns?
Do you long for a friendly, helpful, reliable, confidential service to relieve you of the burden of all those sleepless nights and anxious days?
IT IS HERE! NOW!
Four Corners Middle School is proud to announce that the Nationally Renowned advice columnist
LOUELLA PARSNIPS
will be available to give good and expert advice on any and all of your problems!
TRY HER OUT!
YOU HAVE NOTHING TO LOSE BUT YOUR PROBLEMS!

At the bottom of the notice, in small print:

All letters to be left in the unused locker in back of the broken drinks machine in the corridor by the gym. Answer guaranteed within 24 hours. Complete satisfaction provided or your problems back! (Ha! Ha!)

PS Any attempts at trying to figure out how letters are picked up will result in this service being terminated without further warning.

The notice was printed out really professionally.

It caused quite a stir.

'Louella Parsnips?' Denise DiNovi said. 'Who the heck is Louella Parsnips? I've never heard of her!'

'It says she's a nationally renowned advice columnist,' Andy Melniker said.

'I know that,' said Denise. 'I can *read*.'

'What does *renowned* mean?' Peter Bolger asked.

'It means famous,' Betsy-Jane Garside butted in before I could open my mouth. You know, the way that girl butts in I think she must have a whole lot of *goat* in her family!

On the other hand, maybe it was better for me to keep a low profile right then. I mean, I didn't want people to think I knew anything about that strange and mysterious notice. I wouldn't want people to wonder whether Louella Parsnips might be someone not a million miles away from where they were standing.

Like *me*, for instance!

It was Barbra who first put the idea in my head. Remember she'd said I ought to write an advice column for a magazine? Well, the more I thought about that idea, the better I liked it. But the big problem wasn't setting myself up as an advice columnist. It was getting people to take my advice.

It's a little difficult to get yourself taken seriously as an advice columnist when everyone in your class knows you as Pippa the Jinx. It would be kind of like setting up an airline called 'Plummet USA'. Or a scuba diving company called 'Shark Snax'.

So, the way I saw it, my only option was to go *undercover*!

Here's the plan:

- Louella Parsnips advertises her advice service.
- A whole bunch of people seek her advice.
- Her advice works out really, really well.
- Everyone thinks Louella Parsnips is the hottest property since super-hunk Brad

Rainshaw was signed up to appear in *Spindrift*. (Everyone's favourite day-time soap.)

- Louella Parsnips' mega-fabulous advice becomes the *numero uno* subject in the school.
- Pippa Kane reveals herself to have been Louella Parsnips all along!
- Shock! Gasp! *No! Pippa? Pippa the Jinx?* She's the brain behind the awesome problem-solving power of Louella Parsnips! Gee, you could have knocked me over with a rubberised gym-mat (etc)!
- Pippa is no longer known as *Pippa the Jinx*.
- I get carried shoulder-high through the cafeteria.

Yeah, well, maybe not that last bit, but you get the idea. People stop thinking I'm jinxed and my pals start taking notice of my ideas!

Anyway, back to the crush of people reading Louella's notice.

'If she's so famous, how come I've never heard of her?' Denise asked.

'Maybe she's famous but totally reclusive,' Andy suggested.

'Maybe only the *in-crowd* know about her,' Sophie Carpenter said to Denise with a smug little smile. 'Maybe *that's* why you've never heard of her.'

'Have *you* heard of her, Sophie?' Cindy asked.

'Sure,' Sophie said. 'You mean you haven't?'

Sophie Carpenter is such a total fraud! All of a sudden she was the town authority on a person that I'd only invented the night before.

'I wonder what sort of problems she specialises in,' Stacy said. 'I mean, like school problems? Or personal problems?'

'Maybe family problems,' Cindy suggested. 'Hey – you could ask her to help you with your sister.'

'Huh!' Fern grunted. 'If I have problems – which I never do – I'd walk right up to them and whack them in the kisser. No way would I go to some advice-dork!'

'If I had any real bad problems, I'd go to my mom,' Stacy said.

Cindy shrugged. 'I think it's a good idea,' she said. 'Sometimes it could be useful to get advice from someone you don't know.' She looked at us. 'Not that I'd use her personally myself at all of course ever,' she burbled.

'Like when would it be useful?' Fern asked.

'Like if your best friend smells bad,' Larry Franco said, 'and you're looking for a nice way to tell him.'

‘Hey!’ Nick Arnold said. ‘What’s that supposed to mean?’ Nick was Larry’s best friend.

‘Nothing,’ Larry said. ‘I was just saying.’

‘You said I smell!’

‘I did not!’

‘Did!’

‘Didn’t!’

I thought it was about time I said something.

‘Well, I’d write to her if I had a problem,’ I said.

‘You are a problem,’ Andy said.

I stuck my tongue out at him, which is about all the attention he deserves.

And that was it, really. The bell rang and we all headed off to homeroom.

The big question in my mind was: will there be any letters?

I’d figured that I could afford to slip away from the guys once a day to take a look in the unused locker without anyone getting suspicious. I mean, a person is entitled to go to the bathroom on her own occasionally, right?

The good thing about using that old locker near the gym was that it wasn’t in the kind of area where people usually hang out. Also, I’d see anyone coming down the corridor and I’d be able to disappear before I was spotted.

During morning break and at lunch time I

listened out for people talking about Louella Parsnips. I'd kind of hoped the mysterious 'nationally renowned' advice columnist would be the main topic of conversation. No such luck. In fact, the only person who mentioned her at all was Sophie Carpenter – and I couldn't *believe* all the stuff she was making up about Louella! I mean, she even said her mom had met Louella Parsnips at a high-class function in Indianapolis!

That girl is lucky she doesn't have Pinocchio's problem, or the person sitting across from her in the cafeteria would have been pinned to the wall by her suddenly super-expanding nose.

Meanwhile, I had a slight problem with Barbra.

'Mom found her lipstick,' she sighed. 'The top had come unscrewed and Aurora Crimson lipstick had gotten all over her best lace underwear.' She looked anxiously at me. 'She didn't realise it was *my* fault, but you're going to have to come up with another way of saving me from the kissing thing, Pippa. If her lipstick keeps disappearing, she's going to get suspicious, I think.'

'Leave it with me,' I said.

'Of course,' Barbra said, 'I guess I could

always write a letter to Louella.' She looked at me. 'What do you think?'

'Yeah,' I said slowly. 'You *could* do that. But I think I'll be able to come up with something. Don't worry about it.'

'Hmm, if you say so,' said Barbra. She didn't sound totally convinced.

Heck, I hadn't been expecting that! Now I was in competition with *myself* to solve Barbra's problems. And Barbra was the only one who believed in me in the first place! Rats, rats and triple rats!

'And there's still the thing about the *clothes* she makes me wear,' Barbra sighed, yanking at a lime-green chunky-knit sweater that fitted her about as well as a mouldy mammoth-skin coat would fit a greyhound.

'Don't sweat it,' I said with supreme confidence. 'I'll figure something out. Trust me!'

Just before I headed for home, I managed to sneak off to the unused locker in back of the broken drinks machine outside the . . . oh, you *know*!

I didn't really know what to expect.

A letter?

No letters at all?

A whole heap of letters?

There was a folded slip of paper.

Hey, Louella –
  what's your problem?

It wasn't signed.

Well, hardy-har-har, whoever you were! Big joke!

My next visit to the locker was during break the following morning.

There was a letter. In a pink envelope. On it was written:

Louella Parsnips.
Private And Confidenshal.

Hmmm! *Confidenshal*, huh? I guess they meant *confidential*. Maybe the writer wanted some help with their spelling – they sure needed it!

I sneaked off to the bathroom to read the letter.

Dear Louella Parsnips,

I have a real bad problem, which I hope you can help me with. I am crazy in love with Mr Tove, my math teacher. He is just so totally wonderful I can't tell you! My heart feels like it's going to stop every time I go to his class. I hyperventilate every time he passes me in the corridor. It's making me ill. I can't eat. I can't even eat Chinese-style barbecued spare ribs.

People are beginning to notice.

What can I do? Please help.

Yours in desperation,

LOVESICK

Wow! It sure looked genuine enough. Especially the part about the Chinese ribs. I mean, a person would have to be in a really bad way if they couldn't eat Chinese-style barbecued spare ribs!

Sitting there on the edge of the toilet seat in the cubicle and clutching the desperate pink letter, I suddenly understood the awesome responsibility that I'd brought down on myself. Here was a soul in torment – a person in the depths of despair, reaching out a pleading hand. (The responsibility made me come over kind of poetic for a while.)

I had to do something for poor 'Lovesick'. I had to help her.

I folded the letter away safely in a pocket and headed back to class. I sure had a lot to think about.

I met up with Barbra in the corridor.

'You have some lipstick on your forehead,' I

told her.

With a sigh, she scrubbed it off on her sleeve. 'Mayflower Blossom,' she said glumly. 'It's a new shade.' She gave me a pleading look.

'Uh, I'm working on it,' I said. I tried not to stare at her sweater. Red and blue hoops. It made my eyes go funny if I looked at it for too long. Where did her mom *get* these things? Some kind of home for insane knitwear designers?

'Pippa, are you paying attention?'

I snapped out of my daydream. 'Yes, Ms Fenwick!'

'In that case, would you like to answer the question, please?'

'Oh. Uh. Yeah. Sure thing.' I didn't have the faintest idea what she was talking about. I'd been totally preoccupied all morning with trying to come up with an answer for 'Lovesick'.

Fern whispered something to me.

'Oh! Tom Hanks!' I said.

A few people giggled. Fern groaned.

Betsy-Jane Garside threw her hand up and wriggled like a pig on a thumbtack.

'Yes, Betsy-Jane,' Ms Fenwick said. 'Maybe *you'd* like to tell us whose name appears first on the Declaration of Independence.'

'It's John Hancock,' Betsy-Jane simpered.

'Correct,' said Ms Fenwick. 'Well done, Betsy-Jane.'

'I knew that!' I said. I glared at Fern. 'Why did you tell me Tom Hanks?' I hissed.

'I *said* John Hancock!' she hissed back. 'You need a hearing aid!'

It seemed that being a nationally renowned advice columnist, even one whom Sophie Carpenter's mom had met in Indianapolis, was going to be a lot more tricky than I'd anticipated.

One of the problems with meeting up at Stacy's house is that sometimes we have to put up with all the noise that comes from Amanda's room. When she has the whole Bimbo Brigade up there, it sounds like feeding time in the monkey house at the zoo. (The Bimbo Brigade is Amanda and her three dimwit pals, Cheryl, Rachel and Natalie.)

But the good thing about meeting up at Stacy's is that, if he's not napping, we get to play with Stacy's baby brother, Sam. I like playing with Sam. He's really cute. Now, I'm not saying I'd want a baby brother of my *own*. I'm real happy with the way things are at home right now: just Mom and me. (Dad being home would be nice, except I know they'd be arguing all the time, so I guess that's not an option. Sigh!)

My opinion about babies is this: they are a whole lot of fun in small doses. Like, if Sam gets stinky or starts bawling or breaks something, we can just hand him back to Stacy and get out of there, yeah? I guess it's kind of like when my grandparents come to stay. I really, really love them, but after a week or so it's nice when they go and Mom and I have the place to ourselves again.

Sam was up and about and we were sitting in a ring on the carpet in the living room playing catch the beanbag. Sam was sitting like a big splodge in the middle of the ring and we'd throw the beanbag (really gently) for him to try and catch. He never caught it, at least, not with his hands. Sometimes, if Fern wasn't being careful, Sam would catch the bean bag with his ear or his nose or his tummy. But he'd just chuckle and squeal and clap his hands together, so I guess he didn't mind.

The funniest times were when Sam followed the beanbag with his eyes as it went over his head and he'd fall over backwards. We'd all laugh, and Sam would squeal and wriggle and dribble and chortle.

I guess Fern was the least into playing with Sam. She's not exactly a baby-person. But Sam liked her *best*! He'd laugh like crazy when she came into the room, and he'd go scooting across the carpet to her on his hands and knees and insist on being picked up. And Fern would be kind of horrified, but she'd pick him up all the same, although you could see she felt really squirmy about it.

I'd been working my brain all day, trying to figure out an answer for 'Lovesick'. This was my first commission. I had to get it right. But nothing I came up with seemed to hit the spot.

Like, you can't tell a person to take a cold shower when they're swooning in math class. And you can't tell her to avoid Mr Tove, either. I mean, it's not like her mom would write her a note: 'Please excuse Lovesick from math class as she's got a crush on the teacher.' Face it – that's not going to happen.

I was in a quandary. (That means I was having real trouble deciding what to do.)

'Hey, guys,' I said as casually as I could in the middle of the beanbag game with Sam. 'Have you ever heard of people getting *crushes* on a teacher?'

'On a *teacher*?' Fern spluttered. 'Wow! If that happened to me I'd have a psychiatrist on permanent stand-by!'

Stacy looked suspiciously at me. 'Which teacher?' she asked.

'Huh?'

'Which teacher do you have a crush on?' she asked. They all stared at me. Including Sam, although that was only because I had the bean-bag.

'No teacher at all!' I said. 'What do you think I am, nuts?'

'You really want us to answer that?' Fern said.

'Look,' I said, 'I do *not* have a crush on a teacher, for heaven's sake! All I said was, have you ever *heard* of people having crushes on their teachers? Sheesh, you guys sure jump to conclusions sometimes!'

'I had a crush on the mailman,' Cindy said. We all stared at her. 'Years ago,' she added. 'When I was eight.' She sighed. 'I totally adored him. I'd wait by the mailbox. I even sent letters to myself so I knew he'd stop by.'

Aha! This was more like it. Maybe Cindy would be able to give me some clue as to what I should tell Lovesick.

'So, what happened?' I asked.

'Oh, we got married and went to live in Bermuda in a beach hut,' Cindy said dreamily. 'And he'd take me out water-skiing every day, and we had extended vacations in the Swiss Alps and we had our own yacht and –'

'On a mailman's salary?' Fern interrupted. 'I don't think so!'

'He won the lottery,' Cindy said.

'Yeah,' Fern said. 'I guess that would do it.'

'But what *really* happened?' I said, trying not to sound impatient. 'How did you get over it?'

'Why are you so interested?' Stacy asked, peering at me. 'Are you totally *sure* you don't have a crush on a teacher? You can tell us, you know. We're your pals. We won't make fun. Honest.'

'Hey!' Fern said. 'Don't make promises I can't keep.'

I rolled my eyes, and tossed the beanbag for Sam. 'I'm *interested*, that's all,' I said. 'Forget I mentioned it if it's such a big deal.'

Sam rolled over backwards and squealed with delight.

'He stopped working on our street,' Cindy said. 'I guess he was given a new route. The next time I saw him was about a year later, I think. But it was too late by then. I wasn't crazy for him any more.' She smiled ruefully. 'I couldn't even remember why I'd been crazy for him in the first place.' She shrugged. 'Strange, huh?'

Thanks, Cindy! Big help! So, Lovesick would have to wait until Mr Tove stopped teaching her. Great!

'Amanda had a crush-type-thing on Mr Townes last year,' Stacy said, as she tossed the beanbag again. Sam grabbed for it, missed, and rolled over again with a piercing squeal.

'How'd she get over that?' I asked.

'He gave her a real bad end-of-term grade,' Stacy said. 'That cured her, no problem.'

'Mr Townes?' Fern said with a shudder. 'How could *anyone* . . .? I mean . . . yuck! He looks like a toad!'

Zing! A lightbulb popped on in my head. That was *it*! Totally (or 'toadally') without meaning to, Fern had given me the perfect answer for Lovesick!

Dear Lovesick,

Thank you for writing. I was very sorry to read of your problem. It must be very distressing and bad for your health. I think I may have come up with a cure. This may sound strange, but I feel sure it will work.

The thing you must do is to try and imagine Mr Tove as a *toad*. Every time you think about him, imagine he is a toad. All fat and blobby and green and yucky in a heap of mud somewhere. Keep repeating to yourself: 'Mr Tove is a *toad*. Mr Tove is a *toad*!'

I think you'll find that after a very short time you will no longer feel the same way about him at all.

Very best wishes,

Your problem-solving pen pal, Louella Parsnips

Next day, I sneaked off to put my brilliant reply to Lovesick in the locker.

Oh, my gosh! There were three more letters in there for Louella.

Three!

I had nearly worn my brain out just trying to answer one letter. And now I had three more. Still, I couldn't let people down. I crammed the letters into my bag, left my reply to Lovesick and headed off to class.

'Hi, Pippa,' Barbra said. (Sweater report: bright red with knitted-in yellow ribbons and a big yellow smiley-face and 'Happy Day' knitted in under it.) She showed me a lipsticky tissue. 'Cerise Blush,' she said.

'I'm really sorry,' I said. 'I'm . . . uh . . . I'm still thinking.'

'Oh, don't worry,' Barbra sighed. 'It doesn't matter any more. I'm planning on just dying of embarrassment.'

I'd been so busy trying to help Lovesick that I'd forgotten all about Barbra. 'No!' I said with a lot of determination. 'I'll think of something. I promise.'

I decided it was safest to leave reading Louella's letters until I was sure of not being disturbed. Which meant I didn't look at them again until I was safe at home that afternoon. When Mom works afternoons at her college I usually go back with Fern to her parents' store, unless we have a gang meet. Gang meets nearly always take place at Stacy's house.

But this was one of the afternoons when Mom was home from college early. She was busy working at the computer. (I forgot to mention – I printed up Louella's poster on the computer to make it look really professional.)

'There's guacamole and tortilla chips in the kitchen to snack on,' she called from her office. (It's a spare bedroom, really, but it's usually crammed with all her work stuff so we call it her office.) 'Real food later, honey. I have about two hours' work to do first.'

'OK,' I called.

Perfect! Mom was busy. That meant Louella could get to work.

I carefully closed my bedroom door. I cleared a space on my desk. I opened my notepad so I could make notes. I tore open the first envelope.

Dear Louella,

I wonder if you can help me? My mom is kind of old-fashioned sometimes, and she hardly knows a thing about fashion. For instance, she insists that I wear my skirts so the hem is just above my knees. Now, you only have to take a look around the school to see that these days girls are all wearing their skirts way higher than that. I tell my mom this, but she won't listen. Can you help?

By the way, you met my mom once, although you may not remember her because I guess you meet a whole lot of people.

Yours hopefully,

Sophie Carpenter

So! Sophie 'my-mom-knows-Louella-Parsnips' Carpenter needed some help, huh? How very *interesting*! Yeah, I'd enjoy replying to that letter.

I read the next one. It was really short. I stared at the almost unreadable scrawl.

Dear Louella Parsnips,

My boyfriend ignores me. What am I supposed to do?

J.

PS He doesn't think he's my boyfriend.

I made a note in my pad. I'd already headed one page 'Fashion Problems'. Now I turned over another page and wrote: 'Boyfriend Troubles'.

My plan was to start a new page for every type of problem, then make notes on each problem I solved. That way, if a problem came up twice, I could check back on what I'd said before. Professional, or what?

I opened the final letter.

I recognised the writing straight away.

I looked at the bottom of the letter. It was signed 'Flash'.

Well, 'Flash' might think she was keeping her real identity a closely guarded secret, but I knew exactly who she was.

Believe it or not, that third letter was from Fern!

Fern wanted a dog. That was what the letter was all about. She wanted Louella Parsnips to come up with some way for Fern to kid her folks into letting her have a dog.

Actually, I already knew that Fern wanted a dog. A person couldn't be Fern's friend for most of her life *without* knowing that she really, really wanted a dog. A few Christmases back, when she still wrote letters to Santa Claus, she'd always put 'A DOG, PLEASE' at the top of the list.

Santa left her a stuffed toy dog one year.

The following December her note was headed: 'A *REAL* DOG, PLEASE'.

She didn't get a real dog. She got a hamster. He was a really cute hamster with his own cage complete with a running wheel, and a little hamster house to sleep in, and special hamster toys to play with, and hamster chewing-sticks for it to chew on. Like Fern said at the time, so far as *hamsters* go, Fido (that's what she called the hamster) was a really top-class hamster. But even a really top-class hamster is no substitute for a dog. That was Fern's opinion. And I have to agree with her.

'Can I take him for walks?' Fern had said.

Well, yes, in *theory* she could have, but she'd have to walk real slow or she'd end up dragging him along like a dishmop on a piece of string. Besides, Fern wanted to look cool when she took her pet for a walk. It's kind of difficult for a person to look *totally* cool towing a hamster along the sidewalk on a leash.

'Can I throw sticks for him?' Fern had asked.

Again, in *theory*, why not? She could take Fido to the park. She could let him off the leash. She could find a stick. She could throw it. She could even yell 'Fetch! Fido!' But the chances of Fido going bounding through the grass after the stick would be pretty remote, in my opinion. And the chances of Fido being able to bring the stick back would be around about zero. I mean, it's not stuff that hamsters do, is it?

'Could I have rough-house games with him?' Fern had asked.

You see, Fern liked the idea of a big dog that she could tussle and romp with in the yard. Ten seconds of romping with Fido and he'd probably be so flattened-out that Fern would be able to put him back in his cage by slotting him in through the bars.

So, all in all, Fido, cute as he was, was *definitely* no substitute for a dog.

Anyway, Fido died of old age earlier this year. We buried him in a nice, secluded corner of Fern's back yard. Fern's dad suggested she go buy a replacement. Fern suggested buying a dog instead. Her dad joked that a dog wouldn't fit in the cage. Fern said she didn't plan on keeping the dog in 'that dumb cage'. Somehow the joke turned into a full-scale argument and Fern was told that no way could she have a dog.

Fern's parents run a general store. You know, the kind of place that sells everything from ice cream to charcoal and from TV dinners to refuse bags. Her mom and dad both work more or less full time in the store, which is open twelve hours a day, seven days a week. They have part-time counter staff, but even when they aren't actually serving in the store, they are stocktaking, or labelling stuff, or taking the van to the wholesaler's, or doing accounts, or busy with a whole heap of other miserable stuff like that. This is the reason they said Fern couldn't have a dog. Who'd look after it all day?

Her mom suggested a cat instead.

Fern didn't want a cat. 'Cats are useless!' Fern said to us afterwards. 'What can you do with a *cat*?'

'A whole heap of things,' Stacy had said, offendedly. Stacy is crazy about her pet cat, Benjamin.

Fern had been kind of quiet recently about the dog. I figured she'd given up. Maybe this letter to Louella Parsnips was her very last, final, do-or-die, get-a-dog-or-bust attempt.

She was relying on me. I *had* to come up with a plan. I put my very best thinking cap on.

Half an hour later my very best thinking cap was still in neutral.

Rats! Rats! Rats!

I decided to answer the other letters first.

Dear Sophie,

I have the perfect solution to your problem. Each morning, cut half an inch off the hem of your skirt. Your skirt will get shorter so slowly that your mom will not notice. By the time she notices, you can say something like, 'It must have shrunk in the wash!'

Yours problem-solvingly,

Louella Parsnips

PS Yes, of course I remember meeting your

mom. It was at a gala event in Indianapolis.

You can bet I had a real good giggle over that. I could just imagine Sophie hacking her skirts to pieces bit by bit. And the PS would confuse the life out of her!

But then I put the joke reply to one side and wrote out a proper answer. After all, I had Louella's reputation to think of. The last thing I needed was for Sophie Carpenter to be running around the school telling everyone she'd been given totally useless advice.

Dear Sophie,

By far the best way to remain fashionable at school without getting into arguments with your mom is to do the following. Once you are out of sight of your mom in the morning, roll your skirt up over and over at the waist. Your sweater will disguise the bulge around your middle and your skirt can be elevated to whatever height current fashion trends insist on.

Yours question-answeringly,

Louella

PS Yes, of course I remember meeting your mother. It was at a gala event in Indianapolis.

There! That was it. Maybe it wasn't as much fun as the other reply, but it was pretty darned smart advice, if you ask me.

And while I'd been writing it, I'd had a sudden burst of inspiration about Fern's problem.

Dear Flash,

If your heart is absolutely set on having a dog (which I can tell it is), and if all the usual channels of persuasion have been exhausted, then maybe some direct action is called for. Teddy Bartholemew's dog had puppies recently. The pups should be twelve weeks old now and ready to leave their mom.

Why don't you see if Teddy will let you have one of the puppies? Then you take it home. Once your folks are presented with the dog, their hard hearts will melt and they will not feel able to reject it. Especially (and this is the really cunning part) if the dog just *appears* and is not brought in by you. You can then tell them that 'fate' brought the dog to them!

I hope this solves your problem,

Louella

I felt like writing a PS: 'By the way, if you have any further problems why don't you ask your friend Pippa? I hear she gives very good advice.' But then I thought better of it. Kind of obvious, huh?

'Pippa! Food, honey!' my mom called from the kitchen.

Wow! I hadn't realised how the time was running away with me. I'd been working on those problems for *two hours*! I still had my homework to do. I hadn't even changed out of my school clothes. Louella Parsnips was kind of taking over my life.

'Coming!' I called.

It would be worth it. A couple more weeks of giving ace, *numero uno*, brilliant mega-helpful advice to the guys at school and I could tear aside the mask that is Louella Parsnips and stand revealed as the jinx-less Pippa! Bliss!

We had home-made lasagne for dinner. When my mom works late at college we tend to grab stuff out of the freezer, but when she can get home early – which is usually two or three times a week – she always makes something from scratch.

I haven't really introduced my mom yet, have I? She's very tall (just like me!) and she has long straight hair (just like me). Her hair is mostly black but with occasional grey strands which she refuses to dye. She's a total intellectual (just like me again!) and by twenty million miles the smartest person I know. But she's not *only* mind-bogglingly brainy, she's really practical as well – she even knows how to fix our car when it goes wrong (unlike me).

When she's working she wears half-moon glasses on a cord. She has this way of peering at you over them that makes you feel like she can see right inside you and figure out exactly what you're thinking. I know some people tell fibs to their moms, but you could never get away with it with my mom. She'd just *know*, straight away.

I realise that Dad and Mom still like each other, even though they don't live together any more. In fact, Mom says that they like each other a whole lot better now they *don't* live together, which is a little weird if you ask me. The problem was that they both had important careers (Dad is a mathematician, by the way) and somehow they couldn't quite hold everything together. That's what they told me, anyhow. But they said that the important thing for me to remember was that they both still really loved me. I guess that helped. A *little*.

Mom is a mega-important person at her college, and people are always asking her to do special guest lectures on topics like 'The Semiotics of Aboriginal Culture' or 'The

Anthropological Puzzle of the Mayan Diaspora'. (Just don't ask!) In fact, my mom has even had a book published, she's *that* smart. But that doesn't mean she isn't a totally brilliant mom, too, because she is.

We're always going places together, like art galleries, and the theatre and concerts, and our favourite thing is curling up together on the couch and just *talking*, you know?

It's weird, because when I tell people how much we talk, they usually say: 'What do you talk about?' And I say, 'Oh, just *stuff*, you know?' I don't think other people talk much to their folks. But then my mom is kind of *super-special*.

In fact, I thought as I headed down to the kitchen, my mom is *so* super-special-smart that she might be able to help me with the third of my problem letters. Remember – the girl with boyfriend trouble?

Dinner was on the table. A big dish of lasagne and a bowl of Mom's green salad with her own secret-recipe dressing.

'You haven't changed your clothes,' she said. I usually got out of my school outfit within ten seconds of hitting the house.

'I've been too busy,' I said.

'Uh-huh? Doing what?'

'Oh, just stuff.' I schlooped some lasagne on

my plate. 'Thinking and stuff. Did you get all your work finished?'

'More or less.'

'Mom?'

'Yes, Pippa.'

'If you knew a boy . . . uh, a man, I mean, who you really liked, but you thought he wasn't paying you enough attention, how would you get him . . . uh . . . *interested*?'

Mom peered at me over her glasses. A big grin spread right across her face.

'Who is he? Anyone I know?' she asked.

'Excuse me?'

'The boy,' Mom said. 'The boy you really like but who doesn't know you like him.'

'That's not what I said. And anyway, I'm not talking about *me*!' I screeched. 'Really! A person can't ask a simple hypothetical question in this town without people jumping to totally wrong conclusions!'

'OK, Pippa,' my mom said. 'Calm down.' She grinned. 'I just thought maybe you were trying to tell me something.'

'No, I wasn't,' I said. 'I was asking a hypothetical question.'

'OK, honey. Go right ahead.'

'All right. If a hypothetical girl really liked a hypothetical boy, but the hypothetical boy wasn't paying the hypothetical girl enough attention, what should the hypothetical girl do to let the hypothetical boy know she wanted him to notice her?'

Mom grinned. 'Hypothetically?'

'Yes. Exactly.'

Mom leaned back and gazed up at the ceiling. Mom does a lot of ceiling-gazing when she thinks.

'Well, there's no reason why a girl shouldn't be really upfront about it,' she said. 'For instance, she could invite him to some special event at school. You know, to a disco or whatever.'

'There was a disco just last week,' I said. 'The hypothetical girl might not want to wait until the next one.'

'Oh. OK, then. She could throw a party and invite him and a lot of other people,' Mom said. 'That way it wouldn't be such a big deal if he turned out not to be the boy of her dreams after all.'

'Hmm.' I thought about this. 'It's kind of a lot of trouble to go to,' I said. 'Especially if it doesn't work out. Could you maybe narrow it down a little?'

'She could send him flowers,' Mom said. 'With a cute little poem. You know, something romantic.'

I gave her a dubious look.

She shrugged. 'I don't see why girls shouldn't send boys flowers,' she said.

'You don't?' I said. I could see plenty of reasons why not. Like, you'd look like a total *dork* for a start.

'Certainly not,' Mom said. 'If I was the hypothetical girl, the kind of hypothetical boy I'd want to be friends with would be really pleased to receive a bunch of flowers from me.' She peered at me over her half-moon spectacles. 'And the kind of hypothetical boy who *wouldn't* like a bunch of flowers wouldn't be someone I'd be interested in at all.' She nodded. 'Eat up, honey, before it gets cold.'

I ate up.

When it comes down to it, either you trust your mom's judgement or you don't. And I trust my mom's judgement. So in my reply to 'J.' I told her to send her not-really boyfriend a (small) bunch of flowers with a nice card attached.

I just want you to remember that the business with the flowers was not my idea at all. I just passed it on. 'J.' could have ignored me. I mean, it's not like I *forced* her to do what Louella said.

And I'd just like to mention, for the record, that the *other* thing that happened wasn't really my fault either. If Louella hadn't been so busy coming up with solutions to people's problems then maybe *Pippa* would have had plenty of time to get her homework finished. And if Pippa had finished her homework that night, she wouldn't have been putting the finishing touches to it first thing the next morning.

And then Pippa (that's *me*, folks, in case you're getting confused!) wouldn't have been out in the street before she remembered she didn't have Louella's replies with her.

I zipped back into the house.

'Did you have a nice day at school, honey?' Mom called from her office. (That's Mom being funny – I'd only been gone ten seconds!)

'I forgot something,' I panted as I whooshed up the stairs and into my room. Rats! I hadn't even put the letters in envelopes. I folded Louella's replies and tucked them into envelopes. I scribbled 'J.', 'Sophie' and 'Flash' on the envelopes and headed out again.

What I didn't notice was that I'd put the joke reply in Sophie Carpenter's envelope by mistake. You know, the one that advised her to cut slices off her skirt each day.

Well, come *on*! If someone told you to cut up your clothes, would you do it? Even if the advice came from a nationally renowned advice columnist? Sophie Carpenter had to be some kind of *nut*! Hey, but I'm getting a little ahead of myself. It was a few days later that I found out about that.

OK, let's get this story back on line.

That morning I finally got to meet Barbra's mom.

I'm not sure what I expected. The smears of bright lipstick left on Barbra's forehead put a picture in my head of a mom who would be painted up like a Barbie doll. I had images of stiletto heels and leopard-skin leggings and masses of blonde hair in a huge bouffant. Nightmare mom, in fact.

Mrs Plum was nothing like that at all. She was small and bouncy and super-friendly. She had dark brown, page-boy-cut hair and these huge red-framed spectacles. They had really thick lenses which made her eyes look enormous, like a cartoon person's eyes. In fact, and I don't mean this to sound unkind, Mrs Plum looked exactly like a really cheerful, bouncy cartoon mom!

'Hi, Pippa,' Barbra said.

'Pippa!' Mrs Plum sang out. 'Lovely to meet you. Barbra's told me all about you.' She gave me a big grin. And I do mean big. Barbra's mom had one huge mouth! It only just fitted on her face, it was so big. And right then it was covered with the brightest red lipstick I'd ever seen.

'Hi,' I said. Barbra's sweater was purple and yellow zigzags. It kind of made my eyes water. I figured that if I looked at it for more than a minute or two I'd get a really bad headache.

Mrs Plum's economy-sized smile turned to Barbra. 'Why don't you invite a few of your new friends over some time?' she said. She looked at me. 'Barbra would really love for a bunch of you to come and visit. You could listen to some music. Rent a video. Eat popcorn until it comes out of your ears! It'd be great fun.'

I caught a glimpse of Barbra's face out of the corner of my eye. She didn't look too happy with that idea.

'Mom, there's no room for people to come over,' she said.

'Sure there is,' Mrs Plum said. 'Not for a great huge convention, sure, but there's plenty of room for a few friends.'

Barbra looked at me. 'We live in this really tiny apartment,' she said. 'Maybe we could all go out for a pizza or a burger instead?'

'What? And pay for a meal out when I could make some?' Mrs Plum said. 'That's just silly.'

'Hiya, guys.' It was Fern. 'What's cookin'?'

'Hi, Fern,' Barbra said. 'This is my mom.'

'Hello, Fern,' Mrs Plum said.

'Hi, Barbra's mom,' Fern said with a grin.

'Hey, Fern, you look like the kind of girl who'd go for a home-baked pizza, a rented video and big carton of popcorn,' Mrs Plum said to Fern. 'Am I right?'

'You sure are!' Fern said with an even wider grin. 'Lead me to 'em!'

'That's settled, then,' Mrs Plum said. 'How about this Saturday afternoon?'

And that was that. I could tell that Barbra wasn't too crazy about us going over to her place, but by the time Stacy and Cindy had turned up and been invited as well, there wasn't a whole lot Barbra could do about it.

I made a mental note to find out what Barbra's problem was. After all, most people like to invite their friends home, especially if their mom is going to provide lots of food. But first I had to get my replies over to the unused locker. I couldn't allow Louella Parsnips to let her clients down. People were relying on her! People with skirts that were too long. People without dogs. People with reluctant boyfriends!

I started to have a recurring dream. It was always the same dream. In this dream, I'd be out on the sidewalk in front of our house. I'd have a snow shovel. It would be snowing. I'd be busy shovelling snow off the sidewalk. But the more I shovelled, the quicker the snow fell. I'd be getting nowhere!

I'd clear a patch. I'd look around. It would be covered in snow again. Shovel. Shovel. Shovel. Snow. Snow. Snow. Argh!

I'd shovel away like crazy. There would be lumps of snow flying everywhere, but the snow would just be getting deeper and deeper. It would come up to my knees. Next thing I'd know it would be around my waist.

Around about this part of the dream I'd usually wake up feeling really panicky. I wondered what might happen in the dream if I didn't wake up. Would the snow just get higher and higher until I disappeared under it? Would I be found, weeks later when the thaw came, frozen solid with the shovel still in my hands, like some kind of popsicle? Pippa-on-a-stick!

I told my mom about my dream. She said it sounded like a classic anxiety dream. She asked me whether there was anything worrying me or preying on my mind.

What? Me? No way! I mean, what do I have to be anxious about? It's not like I'm trying to run two separate lives, or anything, is it? It's not like I'm trying to be two different people at one and the same time! It's not like dozens of people are writing to me every day, expecting me to solve their dumb problems!

Well, to be honest, it wasn't *dozens* of people. It just felt like it!

The first letter from Cindy asking about the clarinet practice turned up the same morning that Mrs Plum invited us over to Barbra's home. The second one – the one where she actually remembered to mention her problem – arrived the following morning.

I got ten more letters that week!

Sheesh! Couldn't anyone in this school deal with their own problems?

It was like I'd gone out to shovel a little snow off the sidewalk and I'd been hit by a full-scale avalanche! Yeah, that was what the dream was all about. I was disappearing under an avalanche of problems. My brilliant idea had been too successful. A whole lot too successful for my liking.

Answering Louella Parsnips' mail was turning into a regular industry! I figured I'd have to employ a secretary if this carried on.

Larry Franco wrote that his best friend had the world's smelliest feet, and what should he do about it?

Beats me, Larry. Get a new best friend?

Mariel Poplar wrote that she hated, loathed and despised gym, and could Louella please forge a letter from her mom to get her out of it. She even sent an example of her mom's writing on a shopping list so the forgery would be accurate!

One letter started: 'I will refer to miself as R. G. as I want to be keept annonnymouse . . .'

'R.G.' then went on to whinge that she was totally sure that her bosoms were different sizes. What could she do? Then she signed the letter 'Rachel Goldstein'. Only Rachel

Goldstein (the dumbest member of Amanda Allen's super-dumb Bimbo Brigade) would be dumb enough to sign an anonymous letter! And not only that, but Rachel is built like a bean pole and doesn't have boobs enough to fill a thimble!

I even got a letter from a boy (signed 'X') who really, really liked Stacy Allen and wanted to ask her out, but he was too shy. And he couldn't think of where he should take her either. Could Louella help?

Sure thing, X. In fact, why not leave the whole thing to me? I'll ask her out for you, and why not leave it to me to *take* her out for you, too? Afterwards I'll write and let you know whether you would have had a good time.

Petra Mulligan had spilled ink all over her pillow when she was writing her secret diary in bed one night. How could she get rid of the stain without her mom finding out?

Well, I'll give you one piece of advice, Petra. Don't put that darned pillow anywhere *near* the drier!

Dear Louella,

I have a really difficult problem. I hope you can help. You see, I had this totally brilliant idea. It was that I would set myself up (under an assumed name) as an advice columnist in my school. The plan was to get my friends to realise I was capable of giving really good advice. (They think the opposite!)

Well, the thing is that I'm now getting *twenty million* letters a day with every sort of dumb and stupid problem you could imagine. (One boy asked if I knew how to hook his house up illegally to cable TV, as his parents refused to rent it! I mean, I *ask* you! Some people! I'm not even going to tell you about the liposuction letter – it was too gross to be true!)

Please, Louella, get me out of this!

Yours frantically,

Pippa Kane

Dear Pippa,

Tough cheeseburgers, honey. You got yourself into it, and I guess *you'll* have to dig yourself out!

Yours,

Louella Parsnips

Well, the rest of that week was a total and utter nightmare, I can tell you. I was really glad when the weekend came along and I could relax a little.

The Saturday afternoon at Barbra's place started off just fine. Please note: I *did* say 'started off'!

Fern's dad dropped the four of us off. Barbra lived in the top apartment of a two-storey house. A wooden staircase led up the outside of the house to their front door.

Barbra let us in. The apartment was a whole lot bigger than I'd expected. There was a big, double-sized living room and at least three bedrooms.

Her mom called out, 'Hi, there, everyone!' from the kitchen. 'Make yourselves at home!'

'Where's your room?' I asked Barbra. 'Can we see?' I always like to check out a person's bedroom. It gives you a really good idea of what that person is like.

For instance, Fern's room normally looks

like someone let a Tasmanian devil loose in there just after a hurricane had passed through. My bedroom, on the other hand, is usually pretty tidy with all my books in alphabetical order and all my stuff piled up neatly or put away. That's because I have an orderly mind. Fern has a mind like scrambled eggs that have hit a fan.

Barbra showed us her room. It looked kind of bare. There were no posters on the walls. There was just a bed and a dressing table and a built-in closet.

'The furniture isn't ours,' Barbra explained. 'Our stuff is in storage right now.'

There was a picture pinned to the wall by her bed. A picture of Barbra with her mom and a dark-haired man. It didn't take a genius to figure out that the man was her dad.

(I wish Louella Parsnips could come up with some way to stop people's parents splitting up. That would really be something!)

'Is that your dad?' Fern asked.

'Yes,' Barbra said.

'How long ago did your parents separate?' Fern asked, peering at the picture.

'Two months and three days,' Barbra said.

'Drag!' Fern said.

Fern isn't always the most tactful person in the universe. When my parents split up, I didn't want to talk about it before a lot longer than two months and three days. I didn't even want to *think* about it, that soon!

I thought I'd better change the subject before Fern said something really dumb, like, 'I guess you miss him, huh?' (If Barbra was feeling anything like the way I had felt only a couple of months after my parents separated, that question would have her bawling her eyes out in ten seconds flat).

'Did you rent a video?' I asked.

'Yes,' Barbra said. '*Dumb Like a Fox.* The guy in the store said it was good.'

'That's great!' Fern said. 'My folks rented it last week! It's mega-brilliant! It'll be great to see it again. It's about this high school girl called Tiptree O'Neil, right? Well, her dad is a secret agent for the government, and he's been shadowing these shady foreign spies for, like, months, and –'

'Tell us the plot, why don't you, Fern?' Stacy said. 'That way we won't have to watch it!'

'I won't give any of the good stuff away,' Fern said, flapping her hand at Stacy in a kind of don't-interrupt-me way. 'But there are some really good twists at the end.'

'I smell popcorn!' Cindy said. She was right. The delicious smell of buttery popcorn came wafting into the room.

'Girls!' Mrs Plum called. 'Come 'n' get it!'

We went and got it.

We made ourselves comfortable in front of the TV. Barbra put the movie on. Mrs Plum kept turning up with more popcorn and cans of Coke.

Every time she came in she wanted us to tell her what she'd missed, and while we were telling her what had happened, we'd miss the things that were going on in the movie right then. So we had to keep re-winding in order to figure out who were evil foreign agents and who were the good guys, and who were just innocent bystanders who got sort of caught up in the story. On the whole, the movie was a little hard to follow, with all the interruptions and rewinds and so on.

Fern didn't exactly help, either! 'Oh, that guy is the one who kidnaps Tiptree!' she yelled. 'He's only pretending to be the school caretaker! He's totally *horrible*! At the end he –'

'*Shut up*, Fern!' we all yelled.

'You're messing the whole thing up,' Stacy complained. 'Tiptree hasn't even *been* kidnapped yet, for heaven's sake!'

'Oh yeah!' Fern said. 'Sorry, guys.'

'Just try to keep quiet, huh?' Cindy suggested.

'Yeah. Fine. I won't say another word,' Fern said. 'Oh yeah, I remember now. She doesn't get kidnapped until she's walking home after school. Watch out for the dark blue limo, guys! That's where –'

'*Fern!*'

Watching the film ended up as a near-riot. By the time the good guys and the bad guys were chasing each other with helicopters and motorboats, and Tiptree was hiding out in this big old abandoned factory, whacking the foreign spies with a baseball bat, we were all yelling, 'Look behind you!'

Fern was hollering, 'He's in the closet, Tiptree!' when we weren't supposed to *know* anyone was in the closet.

Stacy ended up sitting on Fern's head. Mrs Plum was laughing so hard that there were tears running down her cheeks. Even Barbra seemed to loosen up a little.

When the movie was finished Mrs Plum put on some really old rock'n'roll records and showed us how to do the twist. (Apparently it was all the rage when her mom was a young woman.) It's not like proper modern dancing, but it was really funny, because while you dance you have to move your feet and your rear end and your shoulders and your arms as if you're trying to screw yourself into the floor.

Mrs Plum went totally bananas, showing us all the neat shoulder moves and arm moves and stuff you could do. Then she collapsed exhausted on the couch and the rest of us had a twist competition with Mrs Plum as judge.

Fern won.

'The trick,' she told us afterwards, 'is to think of yourself as an orang-utan with ants in its pants.'

Yeah, come to think of it, that was exactly what Fern had looked like when she'd been doing the twist – like an ape with an unscratchable itch!

We danced around some more while Mrs Plum went off to the kitchen to fix us some pizzas. Barbra's mom was really good fun to be with. I just couldn't understand why Barbra had acted like she didn't want us to come to her house.

'I think we should have a sleepover party soon!' Stacy suggested. 'All five of us! What do you say, guys?' We all agreed that was a great idea.

'We could do dress-up!' Cindy said.

'We could do dress-up right now!' Fern said. She looked at Barbra. 'Does your mom have any old clothes she'd let us use?'

'I don't know,' Barbra said. 'I guess I could ask.'

The track we were dancing to came to an end and Cindy flopped down in an armchair. 'Yowwww!' she hollered, jumping straight back up. 'Something stabbed me!'

'Oh, sorry,' Barbra said. 'Probably Mom's knitting needles.'

Cindy pulled the cushion aside and, sure enough, there were a pair of really ferocious-looking knitting needles sticking up out of a ball of bright pink wool.

'Booby traps for unwanted guests,' Fern laughed. 'I like it!'

'I'm sorry,' Barbra moaned. 'I thought I'd put everything away in mom's bedroom. I must have missed it.'

Cindy tugged a piece of knitting out from under the cushion. 'What's it going to be?' she asked.

'Something pretty *bright*,' Stacy said, squinting at the colour. She was right. The wool certainly was *vivid*.

'It's a new sweater,' Barbra groaned. 'Mom just won't quit making them for me. She never used to do stuff like that. It's only since . . . since Dad moved out. It's like she's gone knit-crazy! She does it all the time. In her room there's, like, three hundred tons of wool! I'm going to wind up with ten thousand sweaters – and all of them totally *hideous*! It's a *nightmare*!

My mom is making me a total laughing-stock, and she just won't quit! I hate it! You have no idea how much I *hate* it!'

I think we were all a little surprised by Barbra's outburst, but before any of us had the chance to speak, something *really* embarrassing happened.

I heard a small sound behind me. I glanced round. Oh *heck*! Barbra's mom was standing in the doorway with a big plate of pizza slices in her hand. She looked really hurt. I guess she must have heard every word that Barbra had said.

I nudged Fern. She looked round too.

'Oh great!' she said quickly. 'Pizza, everyone!'

Mrs Plum looked straight at Barbra.

'Why didn't you tell me you felt like that?' she said in a very quiet voice.

'You should have *known*,' Barbra said. 'You should have known I hated them! Dad would have known!' And then suddenly she was in floods of tears. She went running out of the room. We heard her bedroom door slam.

There was an uncomfortable silence.

'I'm sorry,' Mrs Plum said to us. 'Things haven't been very easy for Barbra recently.'

'Would it be OK if I went and talked to her?' I said. 'I think I know how she must be feeling.'

That was true. I knew exactly how a person feels when her folks split up. Awful times nine billion!

'I think she'll be better on her own for a little while, thanks, Pippa,' Mrs Plum said. She gave a weak and weedy smile. 'Anyone for pizza?'

Somehow, none of us really wanted pizza right then. But we each took a slice, just to be polite.

After a little while, Mrs Plum went to talk to Barbra in her room.

She came out and told us that Barbra wasn't feeling so good.

Fern called home and ten minutes later her dad arrived in his car.

'Thanks, Mrs Plum,' Fern said as we trooped gloomily out. 'I had a great time . . . uh . . . I mean . . .' She went red. Even Fern realised how inappropriate *that* sounded! 'Uh, I don't mean . . . I mean . . . it wasn't . . . uh . . .'

'Say goodbye, Fern,' I murmured.

'Goodbye, Fern,' Fern mumbled.

'Goodbye, Fern,' Mrs Plum said. 'Don't worry, I know what you meant. Goodbye, girls. Thanks for coming over.'

Like I said, the afternoon at Barbra's place *started* really well!

A Sunday in the Life of a Nationally Renowned Advice Columnist

'Pippa, I'm going to Sellers Market, honey. Would you like to come along?'

'Yes!' I yelled. Then I remembered I had work to do. 'Oh, no! No, I can't.'

Sellers Market is a covered arcade across town. It sells lots of second-hand stuff and antiques and curios and – to be honest – junk. But it also has this really amazing second-hand bookstore. Two floors of wall-to-wall books! Mom and I go there for a good look around about once every two or three months. I've found some really terrific books there in the past.

I have a special set of shelves for my second-hand book collection. I also have a special set of shelves for my 'series' books collections – you know, stuff like the 'Terronvale Twins' series and the 'Juliana Moon, Girl Detective' books. Then, of course, there are my special single-book fiction shelves, and my nonfiction book shelves. Nonfiction is divided into categories by subject; fiction is in author-name order. Second-hand nonfiction has its own section at the end of the first-hand (new) shelf, and second-hand series books are included at the end of the regular books in the same series.

I have all my books catalogued and cross-referenced in a special 'Pippa's Books' folder on the computer. Fern says I'm *obsessed* with my book collection. She says she would never spend all that time and effort on something so totally pointless and boring. It's no good trying to explain to Fern that it isn't pointless and boring at all. But then Fern only has seven books in her collection – and three of those were presents from me! Fern is not big on books.

On the other hand, my mom is the bookiest person in the entire world. The big thing that people notice when they visit our house for the first time is that it is full of books. Books heaped in the hall. Bookcases stuffed full on the landing. Loaded shelves across all the living-room walls, floor to ceiling. (And they totally freak if I show them the boxes of unsorted books that are kept in the basement.)

Basically, my mom and I are really into books, in case you haven't guessed yet. Which was why it was a total pain that I had stuff to do that meant I really couldn't go to Sellers Market.

What stuff?

Stuff like:

Dear Louella,

My feet are way too big. What should I do?

Best wishes,

Clara

And stuff like:

Hey, Louella!

I have a problem. I accidentally phoned a foreign country on my dad's mobile phone the other day. I spoke to some lady in the line at Passport Control in some place called Dubai. She was a really nice lady. At first she thought I was her son, so we had this weird conversation until she figured out that I wasn't her son at all. I thought she was my aunt Stella having fun with me. The problem is that my older sister says that a ten-minute call to a place like Dubai (which she said is in Africa!) would cost a lot of money, and that my dad will totally kill me when he gets the bill at the end of the month. What can I do?

Yours,

Simon Lundy

Yeah, you've got it! Louella was still totally taking over my life. I had a whole batch of letters to answer by Monday.

So, Mom went to Sellers Market on her own and I got down to writing a few helpful replies. (I gave Mom a list of books to look out for. In the 'Karla Kay Investigates' series I still don't have books 2, 5, 7, 14, 17, 18, and 23!)

I turned to a page in my notebook.

The heading was:

Body Parts Problems

1. Bosoms different sizes.

Answer: don't worry about it, it is perfectly normal and these things even themselves out in time. (Answer found in Mom's *FML* magazine. Note: all women's bosoms are slightly different sizes, apparently. Must check this out when I hit the right age!)

2. Nose horrible and frightening to behold. Boyfriend complaining.

Answer: beauty is in the eye of the beholder. If a boy doesn't like you because you have a 'special' nose, then he isn't worth knowing. Find a new boyfriend.

I wrote in a new category:

3. Feet Too Big.

I sat there sucking my pen and wondering what the heck kind of advice you can give to a girl with enormous feet.

Suddenly, there was this really funny taste in my mouth.

The pen had leaked. I had a mouth full of ink!

Bleeeech!

Typical! Just totally typical!

I was on my way to the bathroom with my tongue hanging out to try and keep the vile taste clear of my mouth when the phone rang.

'Hi, there!' It was Fern.

'I can't talk right now,' I told her. 'I have ink in my mouth.'

'Excuse me?'

'Ink!' I hollered. 'Ink from a pen, OK? I'll call back!'

I drank a glass of water. I stuck my tongue out in the mirror. It was purple. So were my front teeth. I tried swilling my mouth out with some anti-bacterial, antiseptic breath-freshener stuff. Yowwwl! *Burny!*

I brushed my tongue with toothpaste. (Don't try it! I nearly threw up!)

I looked at my tongue again. It was mauve now.

Soap and water?

No way!

Dear Louella,

I wonder if you can help me? You see, have a mauve tongue . . .

I tried wiping the ink off on a hand towel. I was very nearly sick again, but judging by the mauve smears on the towel, I must have gotten some of the ink off.

I hid the towel at the bottom of the laundry basket. I tried wiping my tongue with paper tissue. Useless! The tissue just turned into soggy pellets in my mouth.

I looked in the mirror again. Hmm. *Pale* mauve. It still tasted disgusting, though, so I went down to the kitchen and drank a big glass of juice. That helped get rid of the inky taste.

The phone rang.

I picked it up. 'Hello?'

'Oh hi, Pippa, it's Stacy.'

'Hi, Stacy.'

'So, you've been drinking ink, huh?'

Well, thank you, Fern! I wondered who else she'd told in the past five minutes. The local press? CNN?

'No, I have *not* been drinking ink,' I said.

'That's what Fern told me.'

'Fern is one big fibber!' I said. 'My pen leaked, is all!'

'You sound annoyed,' Stacy said. 'What's wrong?'

'My mouth tastes like ink!' I said. 'What else do you think?'

'Whoo! Poetry!' Stacy said. 'Look, we're going to the mall this afternoon. You coming?'

'I can't,' I said.

'Why not?'

'I'm busy.'

'Doing what?' Stacy asked.

'Homework. I'm right in the middle of some homework.'

'So, come as soon as you finish it,' Stacy said.

'It's going to take most of the afternoon,' I told her. 'Sorry.'

'What homework is it?'

'I don't know.'

'Huh?'

'Uh . . . I mean, I haven't checked,' I said quickly.

'You just said you were in the middle of it,' Stacy said. 'How can you not know what homework it is if you're in the middle of it?'

'I didn't mean I was in the middle of *doing* it,' I said. 'I meant I was in the middle of . . . uh . . . *thinking* about *starting* to do it.'

'Let me get this straight,' Stacy said slowly. 'You're in the middle of starting to think about doing some homework, but you don't know what homework it is, although you know it's going to take all afternoon.'

'It's English!' I blurted out. 'I remember now. English.'

'We don't have any English homework,' Stacy said.

'I didn't mean English, I meant . . . uh . . . Oh! Did you hear that? Someone just rang the doorbell, Stacy. I'll have to go.'

'Yeah, but –'

'I really have to go, Stacy. There's someone important at the door.'

'How do you know it's someone important?'

'Sorry?'

'How can you tell it's someone important?'

'Because . . . because they rang the bell in an *important*-sounding kind of way,' I told her. 'Look, I'll see you guys at the mall later if I can get away, all right?'

'Pippa? Are you feeling OK?'

'Yeah. Sure. Why?'

'Well, you sound kind of *confused*. More confused than normal, I mean.'

'Nope,' I gabbled. 'I'm not confused. I just have a whole lot of homework to do. I need to get it finished. I can't come to the mall until it's all done. Where's the problem? Sheesh, I don't know why you're making such a big deal out of this. A person has to do her homework, Fern!'

'I'm Stacy.'

'Sorry, I meant Stacy.'

'Shouldn't you see who's at the door?'

'Huh?'

'You said there was someone important at the door,' Stacy said.

'Yes! There is! I have to go now. See you tomorrow at school, Stacy.'

I had a new dream that night!

In it I was Doctor Pippenstein, and I had created *a creature.* I called it Louella. I put it together on the kitchen table. It was made up of vegetables. It had a pumpkin head with tomato eyes, and a cabbage for a heart, and runner beans for arms and legs, and carrots for fingers.

I was being helped by a fiendish semi-human assistant called Ferngor.

'Ferngor,' I commanded, 'hand me the celery sticks for my creature's feet.'

'I obey, Doctor Pippenstein,' Ferngor said.

When the creature was finished we slid it into the microwave. (Don't ask me how it fitted in there, it just *did.*) Full power for five minutes and it was ready.

We waited with breathless, heart-stopping anticipation while it lay steaming quietly on the table. Would it live? Had I done my calculations correctly? Would all my years of toil and self-sacrifice be proved worthwhile?

The seconds ticked by.

My heart pounded.

Louella didn't move.

Had I failed?

And *then* . . .

Carrot fingers twitched.

'It's *alive*!' I shouted. '*Alive*, I tell you! *ALIVE!!*'

The creature sat up. The pumpkin head turned towards me. The tomato eyes stared into mine. They gleamed. They glowed with intelligence. A runner bean arm reached out. Carrot fingers snatched at me. The tomato eyes glared angrily.

'Gravy!' the creature said. 'Louella . . . is . . . thirsty . . . Louella . . . must . . . have . . . gravy . . .'

I twisted and turned in its vice-like grip.

'I don't have any gravy!' I yelled. 'Let me go! I don't have any gravy!'

'Pippa! Wake up, honey!'

'I don't have any gravy! Let me go! I don't have any gravy!'

'*PIPPA!*'

I woke up.

Mom was sitting on the side of the bed, shaking me. It was Monday morning.

'Ohhh! Wooogh!' I groaned. 'I was dreaming!'

'It must have been *some* dream,' Mom said. She picked up the second-hand copy of *Frankenstein* that she'd found the day before at Sellers Market.

'I knew I shouldn't have let you start reading this book last thing at night,' she said. 'I told you it would give you bad dreams!'

Wow! She was completely right there!

Louella wasn't just taking over my life while I was awake. Now she was messing with my mind while I was sleeping. This whole thing was starting to get out of control!

So, what do you suggest for someone who thinks she has huge feet?

Hey, look on the bright side, when you go on a winter vacation to Calgary, you won't need to hire skis!

Nope, I don't think so.

But not all the problems were that difficult.

Louella wrote to Simon that he should confess about the accidental foreign phone call before the bill arrived. Honesty is the best policy, after all – especially when you're going to get found out anyway! Louella also recommended some *reverse psychology*.

Reverse psychology is when you get someone to do something you want them to do, even though they don't want to do it. Like, if I was to say to Fern: 'You wouldn't dare do so-and-so.' And Fern would say: 'Wanna bet?' And she'd do it. Hey presto! Reverse psychology!

Louella wrote:

. . . You should offer to pay back the cost of the foreign call out of your allowance in weekly instalments. Your dad will be so pleased that you are taking your responsibilities seriously, that he is bound to let you off the payments!

I was walking towards the school entrance when I saw the Plums' car pull up. Barbra got out, looking like someone on their way to a math exam or a disciplinary interview with the Principal. I saw Mrs Plum's face. She didn't look too cheerful either. I guessed that the rest of the weekend over at their place must have been pretty grim.

Barbra shut the passenger door and the car drove off.

It looked like Barbra had got her wish: there was no big lipsticky kiss-mark on her forehead. There was no bright-coloured sweater either. Barbra was wearing a regular dark blue sweatshirt.

The trouble was, Barbra didn't look at all

happy about it. On a scale of one to ten on the happiness chart, Barbra was around minus nine hundred and thirty-eight thousand, four hundred and seventy-two and a half! Approximately.

I went over to her. 'Hi!'

She looked at me. 'Hello, Pippa,' she sighed.

'Are you OK?'

'Not really.'

I decided to inject a little humour into the situation. 'That's a relief!' I said.

She stared at me. 'Huh?'

'Well,' I said, 'if you looked that miserable when you felt fine, I'd be really worried.'

She blinked at me. 'If you say so,' she said. So much for humour.

'You want to go somewhere and talk?' I asked.

'What's there to talk about?' Barbra said. 'I'm the most horrible daughter anyone ever had. I upset everyone. I'm a totally nasty person. I'm the nastiest person in the entire world.'

'No, you're not,' I said. 'You *can't* be. Maddie Fischer is the nastiest person in the whole world.'

'Who's Maddie Fischer?'

'Don't ask. Just take it from me – no way are you anything like as horrible as her.' I looked at

Barbra. 'Has your mom said anything about the sweaters? I couldn't help noticing you don't have one on this morning.'

She nodded. 'Uh-huh.'

'What did she say?' I urged.

'She said I didn't have to wear them if I hated them.' Barbra looked at me. 'But she was really hurt, Pippa. I never meant to hurt her. She must think I'm awful.'

'She won't think that,' I said brightly. 'Believe me, moms *never* think things like that. I mean, when my dad first left home, my mom got really into sewing quilts. That was all she did. Night after night, sewing these little patches of material together. It used to drive me crazy. The whole house was, like, totally covered in these quilts. There was a quilt over the couch, and a quilt on every bed. There were quilts pinned to the walls and people were given quilts as presents. It got so a person couldn't visit our house without staggering out under a double-size quilt!'

'Uh, sorry, Pippa,' Barbra said. 'Are you going somewhere with this?'

'Huh? Oh, yes.' I blinked at her. All I could see were endless heaps of quilts. 'Uh, what was I talking about before I mentioned the quilts?'

'How my mom won't think I'm awful,' Barbra said.

'Yeah! That was it,' I said, remembering. 'The thing is, I was really nasty to my mom about all these quilts. I told her they were a pile of junk and I was sick of tripping over them all the time. Well, we had a bad argument about it. But then when we'd both finished yelling, we sat down and had a long talk – the kind of talk we used to have before Dad went. Mom said that she was making all the quilts as a kind of *therapy*, you know? It was something which helped her to forget how unhappy she was. Anyway, we were both crying and stuff, and I apologised and said she must think I was the worst person in the universe. And she said, "I'd *never* think that about you!" She said, "Moms *never* think things like that." ' I gave Barbra a reassuring smile. 'That was the point I was getting to: your mom definitely won't be thinking you're horrible.'

Barbra was just standing there staring at me.

'What?' I asked. She looked like someone had just hit her over the head with a brick and she was waiting to fall over.

'Pippa, you're a genius!' she murmured.

'I am?' I said. I looked at her. 'Uh . . . how?'

A huge great smile went beaming across Barbra's face. 'Thanks, Pippa! I feel a whole lot better now.'

'Good.' Weird! 'Uh, glad to be of service.' I

couldn't figure why she was feeling better. It wasn't like I'd given her any advice or anything.

Still, if Barbra was happy, that was fine with me.

But I couldn't help wondering what I'd said.

Something strange and a little worrying happened at lunchtime.

The five of us (the Pippagonquin Club, that is, and Barbra: Temporary Honorary Member) were at our usual table, talking about this and that, the way you do.

Cindy was just telling us a horror story about her twin brothers, Denny and Bob. They're seven. They're an absolute nightmare! In fact, they're so completely terrible, that I'm not even going to tell you what they did to Cindy.

I mean, how would you like it if your evil little brothers put all your underwear in the freezer?

Anyway, Cindy was just explaining to us what it feels like to put on a pair of frozen underpants first thing in the morning (in more detail than I *needed*, to be honest), when there was all this noise from the other end of the cafeteria.

The doors burst open. A boy called Lester Fleming came running in, yelling his head off.

Everyone stopped eating and talking and just stared in amazement.

A girl called Jennifer Thompson was chasing after him. She was clutching a mashed-up bunch of flowers. Bits of leaf and chunks of petals fell off the bunch as she waved them at him.

'Lester! Lester! Stop!' she yelled. 'I just wanna talk to you! I thought you'd *like* flowers!'

'Get her off me!' Lester hollered. 'Get that crazy girl off me!'

He high-tailed it out through the exit doors. Jennifer went barrelling after him, shedding flower heads and screaming for him to stop. The exit doors went flap-flap-flap.

There was a second of stunned silence then everyone began to laugh and talk at once.

'What the heck was that?' Fern gasped.

'Didn't you know?' said someone from a nearby table. 'Jennifer has had the hots for Lester for the longest time!'

There was more laughing.

'I guess she finally flipped!' someone said. 'What kind of idiot gives a guy *flowers*?'

I stared at the exit doors.

You know, I had the strangest feeling that I'd just learned who 'J. with-the-boyfriend-who-ignores-her' was.

Oops!

Oh, by the way, there were another two letters in the locker that morning. A boy with volcanic zits and a girl with an annoying little sister. (The girl with the annoying sister signed herself 'A.' She wanted to know how to deal with a pesky little kid who keeps interrupting you while you're talking on the phone. Hmmm! Now then, I wonder who 'A.' could *possibly* be? 'A.' for Amanda, maybe?)

Something else happened the same afternoon.

We were in math class.

Now, I don't have a problem with math. Numbers add up and divide and multiply just fine for me. I guess it's because my dad is a mathematician. Fern, however, totally *loathes* math. In fact, right then Fern was in trouble with Mr Tove on account of some bad homework.

'Fern,' he said patiently. 'How are you going to survive if you can't even do simple things like taking one number away from another without getting it wrong?'

'I'll use a calculator,' Fern said.

'And what if you don't *have* a calculator?'

'I'll ask Pippa,' Fern said, cool as a cucumber.

'And what if Pippa isn't around?' Mr Tove asked, a little less calmly.

'She always is,' Fern said. 'We do everything together.'

Mr Tove went a little pink. He does that when he gets annoyed. 'Well, let's imagine Pippa can't be with you for once,' he said.

'Why not?' Fern asked.

'Because she has the flu,' Mr Tove said.

'Oh, right.' Fern thought for a few seconds. 'I know!' she said. 'I'd borrow my dad's mobile, then I could call Pippa at home!'

Mr Tove gave up on Fern.

People do.

'I need a volunteer to hand out some papers,' Mr Tove said.

Denise DiNovi jumped up. She always sits right at the front for math. I'd never really thought about it before then.

'Good girl, Denise,' Mr Tove said, handing her a sheaf of papers. 'One page each, please.'

'Yes, Mr Toad,' Denise said.

There was a short silence.

Three things happened in this short silence:

1. Denise went as red as an over-ripe tomato.
2. Mr Tove went pink.
3. I figured out who 'Lovesick' was.

There were a few stifled giggles.

'I need to use the bathroom,' Denise croaked. She crammed the papers into Mr Tove's hands and just *fled*!

I felt kind of glad that Denise didn't know the true identity of Louella Parsnips. Denise DiNovi is the sort of person who might not see the funny side of an episode like that. In fact, she's the sort of person who might think the whole thing was Louella Parsnips' fault for telling her to think of Mr Tove as Mr *Toad*. She might, in fact, beat Louella Parsnips to a pulp!

It was a good thing no one suspected the truth!

It was one of those afternoons when my mom was working late at college, and I was planning on going back to Fern's place for a while. I met up with Fern as usual, by the lockers.

She hooked her arm in mine and towed me along the corridor. 'We're going to take a little detour on the way to my place this afternoon,' she said.

'Why?' I asked.

'You'll see.'

We hit the street.

'Are we going to the mall?' I asked.

'Nope.'

'Stacy's house?'

'Does this look like the way to Stacy's house?' Fern asked.

'Not particularly,' I said, 'but you might be taking the scenic route.'

'There's a scenic route in this town?' Fern said.

'Are we going to Cindy's house?' I asked.

'No.' We crossed the road. I didn't have a clue where we were heading. We turned a corner.

'I've heard,' Fern said with a grin, 'that Denise DiNovi has the absolute hots for Mr Tove. Can you believe it?'

'I guess,' I said as noncommittally as possible.

'Rosie told me that she found Denise blubbing in the toilets after math this afternoon,' Fern continued with relish. 'And Rosie said that Denise said that she'd called Mr Tove "Mr *Toad*", because she was crazy in love with him. Isn't that something?'

'I guess,' I said.

'Kind of *weird*, though,' Fern said thoughtfully. 'Why call Mr Tove "Mr *Toad*" if she's crazy in love with him?'

'I guess she was confused,' I said. 'Love does weird things to your mind.' I looked at her. 'So I'm led to believe,' I added hastily.

'Yeah, I guess it does.' Fern shook herself. 'Yeccchhhh! Mr *Tove*?'

'Fern? Where are we going?'

'Nowhere.'

'Huh?'

'We're *here*!'

I didn't recognise the house. Fern led me up the side like we were a couple of secret agents or something. We came to a side door that led to the back yard. Fern put her ear to the door.

'Fern?' I said.

'Shhh!'

'What are we doing here?' I whispered.

'Wait!' she whispered. She lifted her fist and knocked softly.

Knock. Knock-knock. Knock-knock-knock.

A knock answered from the other side of the door.

Knock-knock-knock. Knock-knock. Knock.

'That's the signal,' Fern said.

The door opened. Teddy Bartholemew's freckly, lemon-shaped face appeared.

Something moved lower down near the ground. It was a puppy. A golden retriever puppy. It squiggled and wriggled to get out through the gap where the door was slightly open.

'Have you brought it?' Teddy asked Fern.

'Sure,' she said. 'Here.' She took something out of her bag and handed it over to Teddy. It was a virtual pet. (Her folks had bought it for her last birthday – another dog substitute, would you believe?)

'Uh, what's going on here?' I asked. I had the strangest feeling I knew exactly what Fern and Teddy were doing. Following Louella Parsnips' instructions! But Louella hadn't meant for Fern to sneakily sneak off with one of the puppies without Teddy's folks knowing. That hadn't been the idea at all. I mean, isn't there a law about puppy-napping?

'Swapsies,' Fern said to me. 'Trust me, I know what I'm doing. One *virtual* pet for one uh . . . whatever the opposite of "virtual" is.'

'Real?' I suggested.

'Yeah! That's the word.'

I looked at Teddy. 'Do you have permission from your mom and dad to do this?' I asked.

He shrugged. 'They'll never notice one missing,' he said.

'I think they *might*,' I pointed out. 'Don't you think you should at least tell them?'

'Pippa,' Fern said, 'don't be such a party pooper. Trust me, I've consulted an expert about this. It'll all be fine.'

'Fern! I never meant for you to –' Erk! I clamped my mouth shut. I'd nearly given the whole game away!

'What?' Fern asked, frowning at me.

Fortunately, the puppy chose that moment to wriggle through the gap between the door and the doorpost. It went scooting between my feet, trailing a skinny leash.

'Catch him!' Teddy squealed. 'Don't let him run into the street!'

Fern did a magnificent flying tackle on the

leash and the puppy was yanked to a stop. It did a couple of spectacular somersaults and bounced on its backside, but it didn't seem to mind. I guess puppies are made of rubber! It just sat there, all tongue and gangly legs and huge paws and floppy ears.

Fern scooped the puppy up in her arms. It licked her face with a tongue like a couple of yards of pink flannel – *schluuup, schluurpp, schluuuurrrrppp*! 'Bad boy!' she said, not sounding like she meant it at all. 'Mustn't run away! Bad, bad boy!' The puppy's tail was spinning like a helicopter's propeller. Any faster and I could imagine the two of them lifting clean off the ground and flying off over the rooftops.

Teddy closed the door.

'This is crazy,' I told Fern. The puppy was wriggling in her arms, wanting to go down. 'Teddy's folks are guaranteed to notice one of their puppies is missing. I mean, it's not like he's just some mutt, Fern.'

'It's cool,' Fern said. 'Chill out, Pippa.' She kissed the puppy on its domed head. 'I'm going to call him Jefferson Airplane.'

'You're going to call him wha-at?'

'Jefferson Airplane. They were this totally cool rock group that hung out in San Francisco.' Even though Fern had never been to San Francisco, she always though of it as her 'spiritual home'.

'That's too long a name,' I pointed out.

'Well, Jeff for short,' Fern replied. She put the puppy down. He scampered off, towing Fern along in his wake. I trotted along beside her.

'I have this totally brilliant plan, see?' she said. 'I'm going to tell my folks I found Jeff running loose in the streets. I'm gonna say, "Hey, I have an idea, guys." Then I'm going to suggest we look after Jeff *temporarily* while I ask around the neighbourhood for anyone who has lost a dog, right?' She grinned sneakily. 'Except, of course, that I'm *not* going to ask around at all! Once Jeff settles in, my folks won't have the heart to throw him out. Get it? Everyone's happy! Teddy has that dumb virtual *pest* thing. And I have a dog – at *last*!' She tapped the side of her head. 'And all thanks to *brains*, the wonder head-filler!'

'You came up with this whole plan on your own, huh?' I asked.

'Sure did. Stacy's not the only one who has smart ideas, you know!'

'I guess not,' I said. I glanced at her. 'Uh, if I had come up with an idea like that –'

'Which you didn't!'

'No. That's true,' I said. 'But if I *had*, I don't

think I would have taken the puppy without Teddy's folks knowing.'

'Yeah, well, don't take this wrong, Pippa,' Fern said with a smile. 'But what you know about good ideas could be fitted in a bug's bum-bag and still leave room for a skyscraper. Know what I mean?'

'Hmmph!'

The journey to Fern's house was kind of interesting. Fern was talking nonstop about all the amazing things she and Jeff were going to do. All the fun they were going to have together. How she would teach him to beg and roll over and walk to heel. Jefferson Airplane didn't behave like walking to heel was one of his priorities. He had his own ideas about which way he wanted to go, and those ideas didn't always fit in with what Fern wanted. There was quite a lot of dragging and pulling needed to keep Jefferson on route.

Every now and then he'd catch a whiff of a totally *brilliant* smell and Fern would be dragged off sideways. Then he just *wouldn't* move until he'd had a real good nose-full.

'Jefferson!' Fern said sternly. 'Will you behave!'

Jeff grinned and wagged his tail and let his tongue hang out the side of his mouth. Judging by the look in his eyes, I guessed he was thinking. 'Behave? Come *on*! I'm a puppy!'

Eventually we got to the corner of Fern's street.

The Kipsaks' general store is halfway along the street. Next to it is a patch of unused ground leading right to Fern's house. Real handy, huh? My mom says she wishes her college was that close to our house. She'd be able to spend an extra hour in bed in the morning.

The store is called 'The Kip Sack'. It's one of those stores that has a whole lot of stuff set up on the sidewalk outside – special offers and bargains and things like that.

'OK, here's the deal,' Fern said. 'We *found* Jeff running around in the road, right?'

'Uh, Fern?'

'He was in real danger of getting squished by traffic, right?'

'Umm –'

'So we had to grab him and bring him here. Got it?'

'What about the collar and leash?'

'What about them?'

'If you're trying to make like he's a stray,' I explained, 'he shouldn't be wearing a collar.'

'Excellent point, Pippa!' Fern said. She crouched down and unbuckled Jefferson's collar. She hooked her arm around his belly and kept a good tight grip on him. She handed me the collar and leash. 'Hide these,' she said.

I stuffed them in my bag.

Fern stood up. Keeping a hold on Jefferson was a real job! He knew how to wriggle in five different directions at once.

'Hold still, Jeff!' Fern said as she tried to keep the squirming crazy puppy under control. Jeff grinned and schpluffled and went *schloooo* with his tongue right across Fern's face.

'Spit! Sput! Spootie!' Fern spluttered, all over wet. 'We'd better get this over with pronto,' she said.

I followed her across to the store. This time of day her mom and dad would probably both be in there.

'Fern?' I said as we reached the sidewalk. 'Are you *sure* about this?'

'Whadaya mean?'

'I mean,' I lowered my voice to a hiss, '*fibbing* to your folks.'

'It's only a tiny little fib,' Fern said, keeping her head back to try and avoid getting licked to death by Jefferson Airplane. 'And it's for a good cause.'

I followed Fern into the store.

Her dad was behind the counter, talking to a woman customer. I thought I kind of recognised her, but I didn't have time to think about it before Fern went into her big act.

'Dad! Look what I found!' Fern panted. 'He was running loose! He nearly got run over by a truck!'

'Good Lord!' Mr Kipsak said. He stared at the squiggling and wriggling puppy in Fern's arms. Then he looked at the woman customer. 'Hilary – *look*!'

'I couldn't let him run around like that, could I?' Fern said, acting away like crazy. 'I had to bring him home for his own safety, didn't I?'

The woman customer turned and gazed at the puppy.

That was when I noticed that Mr Kipsak had something in his hand. It was a large white card. The kind that the Kipsaks often put in their window – you know: 'Baby-stroller for sale, one careful owner.' 'Parakeets going cheap.' (Cheep – geddit?) That sort of thing. Personal ads.

The card read:

Golden Retriever Puppies for Sale
Seven 12-week old puppies, all in excellent health. Guaranteed pure-bred. Need good, loving homes.
Call Hilary or Max Bartholemew on:
[followed by a phone number]

Then I suddenly remembered who the woman customer was. I'd seen her at school. She was Teddy Bartholemew's mom.

She stared at the puppy like her eyes were going to explode.

'Fern!' she gasped. 'Where on earth did you find him?'

Before Fern had the chance to draw breath, Mrs Bartholemew yanked Jeff up out of her arms.

'In the . . . on the . . . out in . . . I . . . he was . . .' Fern blabbed.

Mrs Bartholemew held the wriggly puppy up and scrutinised him with narrowed eyes. 'Yes,' she said. 'Yes, it's definitely one of ours. It's definitely one of Lady's litter. But how on earth did he get out?' She stared at Fern. 'In the street, you say?'

'Uh, yeah . . .' Fern looked like someone had just whacked her in the mouth with a ten-pound catfish. 'Out . . . in the . . . street . . .'

'I don't understand,' Mrs Bartholemew said. 'Where's his collar? How did he get out?' She frowned at the puppy. 'You naughty boy! Did you slip your collar and escape?'

'*Wuff, wuff,*' the puppy wuffed happily. *Li-i-i-ick*, went its tongue. *Wag-wag-wag* went the tail.

Fern just stood there with her mouth

hanging open.

'I'm going to have to take better care of you, aren't I?' Mrs Bartholemew said, cuddling the puppy up against herself. She smiled. 'They're just pure mischief at this age. I can't imagine how he got out, the little tinker!'

'But . . .' Fern said. She gulped. I thought I could see tears in her eyes.

Mrs Bartholemew looked at her. 'I'm really very grateful to you, Fern, dear,' she said, smiling. 'You're a good girl. Who knows what might have become of the poor fellow?'

Fern blinked at her. 'But . . .'

Mrs Bartholemew's face fell. 'Oh lord! I hope the others haven't escaped as well. There could be puppies all over!'

'I don't think so,' I said. 'I think we'd have seen them.'

'Yes, yes,' Mrs Bartholemew said. 'I'm sure you're right. Still, I'd better get back and check everything out. Teddy will be worried sick if he gets home to find one of them missing. He absolutely adores them, you know.'

'I bet he does,' I said, trying not to sound too sarcastic.

'But . . .' Fern said softly. 'But . . .'

Mrs Bartholemew tucked Jefferson Airplane under her arm and left the store.

'Well, now,' Mr Kipsak said with a big

smile. 'Aren't you two girls the good Samaritans? I think you deserve a reward.'

He handed us a candy bar each.

Fern heaved a great big, long, heavy, heart-felt sigh. I could see that she was, like, *that* close to bursting into tears. I felt pretty bad about the advice Louella had given, I can tell you *that*!

Oh *heck*, I thought to myself, *Louella lucks out again*. Darn! It was a good idea, too. It was just such a pity it didn't work!

‘Do you know what I’m going to do to that dumb chowder-headed dimwit imbecile Louella Parsnips if I ever meet her?’ Fern said to me half an hour later when we were in her room. She seemed a little ticked off by recent events. She had just told me that the whole puppy business had been Louella’s idea.

(My response: ‘No? Re-e-e-e-eally? You wrote to Louella Parsnips? Wow!’ Great acting, huh?)

‘Uh, no,’ I said. (I couldn’t help being just a little interested in what she was going to do to Louella Parsnips if she ever met her.) ‘What are you going to do to her if you ever meet her?’ I asked.

‘I’m going to stuff my arm down her dumb stupid melonhead throat and pull her feet up through her nose!’ Fern exclaimed. ‘That’s what!’

‘Oh.’ (Ouch!)

‘And then I’m going to yank on her ears until

they're half-a-yard long,' Fern continued. 'And then I'm gonna go someplace where they have those real huge spiky cactus-type plants. Then I'm gonna hang her by her ears on the biggest, spikiest cactus of them all and whistle for the buzzards to come and get her!'

'I see.' (Eek!)

'And then when they've finished gnawing on her, I'm gonna run over her with a road-roller!' Fern snarled, grabbing up handfuls of her bedclothes and twisting and wrenching them in a way that made me feel a little queasy. 'Then I'm going to stomp up and down on her with big boots on! And then I'm gonna scrape up all the bits and mail them to an earthquake zone!'

Fern, in case you haven't noticed, was not a very happy person right then.

Louella Parsnips had become public enemy *numero uno*! Fern seemed to blame her for the fact that Mrs Bartholemew had been in the store that afternoon to have the puppies-for-sale note pinned up.

'How was she supposed to know you'd run right into Teddy's mom?' I said. 'She's an advice columnist, not a psychic! Anyway, if you'd OK'd it in advance with Teddy's folks, like I said you should all along, then –'

'Shut up, Pippa!'

'I was only saying –'

'Grrrr!'

I shut up.

Now then, was this a good time to confess to Fern that I was, in fact, the elusive Louella Parsnips?

What? And be killed? I'd have to be out of my mind!

Dear Louella Parsnips,

You are the most stupid, useless advice columnist in the entire world and I totally, utterly and completely hate you!

Yours,

Sophie Carpenter

PS And you are a total liar, too! You never did meet my mom! She was invited to the function in Indianapolis, but when she saw your name on the guest list she decided not to bother, because you are such a total geek! So there!

That was the only letter in my special problems locker the following morning.

Oh heck, what had happened *now*?

It didn't take me long to find out.

Sophie was holding court in the hallway where we keep our lockers.

'I've been grounded for two weeks!' she was

saying as I arrived. 'Two whole weeks! A person can die of social starvation in two weeks!'

'Why the heck did you do it?' Cindy asked her. 'How did you think you'd get away with it? You must have realised your mom would notice.'

'I thought that if I just cut a half-inch off each morning, the difference would be so small that she'd – I don't know – that she'd just think I was, like, *growing*.'

'By half an inch a day?' Paula Byrne said. 'That's some growth-spurt, Sophie!'

'Well, it seemed like a really neat idea at the time, all right?' Sophie said from between gritted teeth.

The story, as I pieced it together, was that Sophie had cut the first half-inch off the hem of her skirt on Monday morning. Her mom hadn't noticed – at least, not until she came to do the weekly wash on Monday night. She noticed then, OK!

I can just imagine it:

'Sophie! What on earth happened to your skirt?'

'Huh? Oh, *that*. I . . . uh . . . I *improved* it, Mom. Do you like it?'

'Do I *like* it??? Look at it! It's ruined.'

'It's not ruined at all. It's . . . uh . . .

fashionable.'

'Fashionable? You . . . you . . . Urk! Grrg! Frukk! Gaaargh! Grahhhhh!'

'I can tell something has upset you, Mom. How about we sew the missing piece back on, huh? Mom? Would that be OK? Mom? Mom – why are you looking at me like that, Mom? No, Mom, put down that steak tenderiser! Arrgh!'

Well, maybe Sophie didn't get beaten to a wafer with a steak tenderiser, but, if you edit out the violent attack with the kitchenware, I suspect the above is a pretty fair representation of what happened in the Carpenter house Monday night.

I mean, like I said, what kind of a four-alarm mega-bubbleheaded imbecile follows advice to cut her clothes up?

It's a good thing I'm a naturally optimistic person, or I could have gotten severely worried about the way some of Louella's advice was going.

Optimism: An Explanation.

Optimism is the opposite of pessimism. For instance, you arrange a picnic. Optimism is when you say: it'll be a lovely day! Pessimism is when you say: I just bet there'll be bugs, and it'll rain, and we'll all come down with food poisoning from the ham sandwiches.

I read in a book that a good test of whether a person is an optimist or not is to half fill a glass with water.

An optimist will say the glass is half *full*.

A pessimist will say the glass is half *empty*.

That's the idea, anyhow. I tried it on Cindy. 'It's half a glass of water,' she said. I don't know *what* that says about Cindy.

Then I tried it on Fern. She drank the water.

Stacy said: 'It's a really, really weak glass of clear Coke without the bubbles.'

My friends are totally useless when it comes to trying out psychological experiments. I guess I should hang out with guinea pigs.

Cindy and Fern and Barbra and Stacy were already in homeroom when I got there. (I left Sophie ranting and raving in the hallway.) The other three were crowded around Cindy. Cindy was sitting down. She was moaning and rocking backwards and forwards, and every time she rocked forwards her head went *bonk* on the desk top.

(I'd just like to point out at this stage that this is not normal behaviour in our class – not even for Cindy.)

'Is something wrong?' I asked.

They looked at me in silence, all except for Cindy who kept *bonking* her forehead on the desk.

'What's happened?' I asked.

Cindy stopped rocking. She stared at me.

'Never trust an advice columnist!' she groaned. 'Never! Nevernevernever!' *Bonk!* Rock. 'Never.' *Bonk!* Rock. 'Neverever.' *Bonk!* Rock. 'Nevereverever!'

I felt kind of uneasy. I guess in a thriller the writer would say my blood ran cold. What had that dumb cluck Louella Parsnips done now? (Heck, even I was beginning to turn against Louella!)

'Cindy wrote to Louella with a problem,' Stacy told me. 'You know how she hates having to learn the clarinet?'

'Uh-huh,' I said.

'Well, Louella Parsnips told her to . . .'

I tried to act surprised while Stacy told me what Louella Parsnips had written.

'So, uh, so what went wrong?' I asked.

Bonk! Rock. 'Don't ask!' Cindy groaned.

'Her mom heard Devon Palminieri playing in Cindy's room,' Stacy explained. 'And she was so thrilled at how fantastic it sounded, that she's put Cindy in for an interstate talent contest in Mayville next Saturday.'

'Oh, *no*!' I gasped. 'I don't *believe* it!'

Everything was going haywire. What next? Would the girl with the big feet turn up minus her toes? Would 'A.' murder her little sister to stop her butting in when she was on the phone? Would Louella Parsnips be seen running screaming through the corridors of Four Corners Middle School, gibbering and tearing her hair out?

Cindy looked at me. 'What are *you* so bothered about?' she said. 'It's not like *you* have to stand up in front of five hundred people and make a total fool of yourself.'

'Well . . . I . . .' My voice trailed off. 'I . . . it . . . if . . .' I swallowed hard and started again. 'I was being sympathetic, that's all,' I ended lamely. 'Uh, poor *you*!' I tried to look sympathetic and innocent both at the same time. I probably looked like I had stomach ache.

'I think someone needs to find out where Louella lives,' Stacy said. 'And I think they should have a serious talk with her about her dumb advice.'

Fern smacked her fist ominously into her other hand. 'I think someone should punch her out!' she said.

Cindy looked at me. 'You know something, if I didn't know it was impossible, I'd think Louella darned Parsnips was related to *you*!'

I nearly jumped out of my shoes. 'What's that supposed to mean?' I squeaked.

'It means that Louella rotten Parsnips,' Cindy grated, 'is the only person in the world who gives worse advice than you do!'

There was a brief silence.

'Do you want to know what I think?' Stacy said. 'I think that Louella Parsnips isn't a renowned national advice columnist at all. I think she's someone at this school.'

'But . . . but Sophie's mom has met her . . .' I stammered. 'At a function . . . in . . . Indianapolis.'

'Yeah, sure!' Fern said. 'According to Sophie her mom has met everyone from Arnold Schwarzenegger to the Queen of England!'

'Yeah,' Stacy said. 'Plus her mom was the first woman in space and the first woman to paddle across the Atlantic on a waterbed. Not!'

'Gee,' Barbra said, looking at me. 'I wonder who Louella could be?' She lowered her voice. 'Do you think it could be someone in this class?'

I shook my head. 'No way,' I said.

'Well, I think we should stake out that locker in back of the drinks machine,' Fern said. 'And I think we should grab the first person to come within ten yards of it and beat her to death. That's what I think.'

'Yeah! And save a piece for me!' Cindy growled. 'A nice *big* piece!'

Gulp!

LOUELLA!!!

Look at the mess you've gotten me in!

I need some good advice. Like *now*!

I managed to get Barbra alone during morning break. By which I mean I dragged her off into a storeroom when no one was looking. It smelled of bleach and horrible old floor mops.

'You look kind of worried,' she said. 'Can I help?'

I looked at her. I peered around at the shelves full of old school junk, just in case someone was lurking behind the spare washroom towels or the boxes of cleaning fluid. I looked at her again.

'I have a slight problem,' I told her.

'Uh-huh?'

'Are you any good at keeping secrets?' I asked.

'Sure.' She sounded intrigued.

'Even really *big* secrets?'

Barbra licked her finger and made a cross over her heart. 'Nothing you tell me will pass beyond these four walls,' she said solemnly. 'Cross my heart!'

'Six walls,' I said. (The storeroom was L-shaped.)

She looked around. 'Six walls,' she agreed.

I decided to jump straight in with both feet. 'What would you say if I told you I was Louella Parsnips?' I asked.

Barbra stared blankly at me.

'Louella Parsnips?' I said helpfully. 'You know, the advice queen of Four Corners Middle School?'

'Ooh-ee-ahhh-ummm,' Barbra mumbled. 'Ohhhh, oooh.'

I blinked at her. Had I suddenly stopped speaking English? 'Did you get that?' I asked. 'It was me all along. I pretended to be –'

'Yes,' Barbra interrupted. 'I heard what you said. It was just . . .' Her voice trailed off.

'What?'

'Oh. Nothing.' She smiled in a sort of *what-next* way. 'Well!' she said. 'What a surprise!'

I stared at her. She sure was reacting in a bizarre way to my big revelation.

'Thing is,' I said, 'I need help.' I looked at her with anxious eyes. 'I need a whole bunch of help, Barbra. The whole Louella Parsnips idea is sinking big time. You heard that business with Cindy and the clarinet this morning. That's all my fault. Louella gave her that advice.'

'Yes,' Barbra said.

'And Louella is me,' I added, pointing to myself, just in case it hadn't quite sunk in with her yet.

'Why are you pretending to be Louella Parsnips?' Barbra asked.

'So that people will realise I can give good advice,' I said. 'So people will stop calling me Pippa the Jinx.'

'But how were people supposed to know she's you?' Barbra said. She frowned. 'That you're her, I mean.' She looked confused. 'Whichever!'

'I was going to reveal the whole thing at an appropriate moment,' I explained. 'After people had benefited from Louella's brilliant advice for, say, a couple of weeks, I was going to stand up in class and say: "I am Louella Parsnips!" ' I sighed. 'And everyone would have been really amazed and impressed.'

Barbra gazed at me. 'I don't think Cindy will be amazed and impressed,' she said. 'I think Cindy will be totally unamazed and unimpressed. In fact, judging by the way Cindy was acting this morning, I'd say Cindy would probably take her clarinet and beat you to death with it.'

'I know!' I said miserably. 'Don't tell me! And Cindy isn't the only one.'

Barbra tried to hide a smile. 'Sophie Carpenter's skirt?' she said.

I nodded.

'And the girl in the cafeteria yesterday with the flowers?' she said through giggles.

'Uh-huh.'

'Ohmigosh – and Denise! When she called Mr Tove Mr Toad – was that you too?'

'Yerrrghhhh,' I moaned. 'All me. And there's Fern and the puppy as well.'

Barbra burst out laughing. 'Pippa, you total *loon*!'

I plumped down on a box of washcloths. 'What am I gonna do?' I groaned. 'If I confess, I'll just get lynched. I don't want to get lynched. I'm too young to get lynched. I'll never get to be a Supreme Court judge if I get lynched.' I looked up at her. 'That's my big ambition,' I confided in her. 'To be a judge when I grow up.' I heaved a sigh. 'If I *get* to grow up.'

'But why did you give people such awful advice?' Barbra asked.

'I *didn't*!' I said. 'The advice was just fine.' I frowned. 'It's just that . . . I don't know . . . something *stupid* always seems to happen between me *giving* the advice, and the person at the other end actually *doing* what I suggest. It's like some strange and uncanny force intervenes.'

'Like a jinx, you mean?'

'No! Not like a jinx,' I said crossly. 'Nothing like a jinx at all, in fact.'

'Sounds like a jinx to me,' Barbra said mildly.

'Well, it isn't,' I said determinedly. 'It's something else entirely.'

Barbra sat down next to me.

'It stinks in here,' she said.

'I know,' I said. 'It was the only place I could think of where we wouldn't be disturbed by someone wanting to lynch me.'

'Don't panic. Who knows Louella is you?'

'Nobody, I hope – not *yet*,' I said miserably. 'But the way my luck is going, someone will get a letter from Louella confessing the whole thing!'

Barbra looked at me. 'Uh, *you're* Louella.'

'I know.'

'So how could *Louella* write a letter? *You'd* have to write it.'

I nodded mournfully. 'You'd think so, wouldn't you?' I sighed.

'I . . . see . . .' Barbra said slowly, like she was thinking, *Help! Get me out of here! Pippa's gone mental!*

'You don't know what it's like, trying to be two people,' I told her. 'It does strange things to your brain.'

'What I don't understand,' Barbra said thoughtfully, 'is, how come Louella's advice is so awful, when the advice you give to me is really good?'

I looked at her. 'It is?' I said.

She nodded. 'Sure,' she said. 'The shopping idea was brilliant.'

I brightened a little. 'Yeah, it was, wasn't it?'

'Of course, the lipstick thing didn't really work,' Barbra said, bursting my little bubble of self-confidence.

'And I wasn't able to help you with the ugly sweater problem till it was too late,' I said gloomily. 'And now your mom and you aren't even friends!'

'Wrong!' Barbra said. 'You helped me out a whole lot with that.'

'I did?'

'Yeah, sure. I had the longest talk with my mom last night. We talked all night. It really cleared the air. There was all this stuff that we hadn't been able to say to each other for, like, months. Last night we just kind of *splurged*!' Barbra pointed at me. 'And it was all your idea!'

'It was?'

'Yeah. You told me how you and your mom were acting when your dad left home. I realised my mom and I were behaving exactly the same way.'

'Yes, but that wasn't *advice*,' I said. 'I was just talking.'

Barbra laughed. 'Maybe that's the answer, Pippa. Maybe your problem is that you try too hard. Like, when you just *talk*, you make a lot of sense. It's only when you try to be helpful that things seem to go loopy.'

'I see,' I said. 'That's very Zen, you know.'

'*Zen*? What's that? It sounds like a new washing powder.'

'It's a kind of philosophy thing,' I said. 'My mom's really into it. It's a really complicated bunch of stuff, but one of the things that Zen teaches is that you have to go with the natural flow of things. So, like, when I *try* to give advice, it all goes wrong, but when I *don't* try, everything works out just fine.' My chin sank into my hands. 'This is going to be really difficult,' I said. 'How the heck do I try not to try? I mean, if I'm *trying* not to try – that still means I'm *trying*, and if –'

'Do you want my advice?' Barbra interrupted.

'Yes!' I almost yelled. 'I do! I really, really do!'

'Kill off Louella,' Barbra said. 'Kill her off right now.'

'How?' I said. 'Strangle her with my bare hands? Stab her to death with her own advice pen?'

'Nothing so drastic,' Barbra said calmly. 'Pin a notice on the board, saying she's gone on an extended vacation to, uh, to Honolulu due to overwork and brain fatigue brought on by occupation-related stress.'

I sat up. 'I could do that,' I said.

'Sure, you could,' Barbra said. 'Do it right now!'

'No. Someone will see. Besides, I can't get to my mom's computer until this afternoon to print the notice out.' I grinned. 'But first thing tomorrow, that notice is going up! Wow, thanks, Barbra. You're a real pal.' My eyebrows knitted. 'You won't tell anyone about this little talk, will you?'

'Of course not.'

'You *especially* won't tell Fern and Cindy and Stacy, will you?'

She looked at me. 'Uh, no,' she said slowly. 'I *very* certainly won't tell them.'

I breathed a sigh of relief.

That was the answer! Send Louella off on a long, long vacation. Honolulu would do just fine – unless I could think of some place that was even more remote!

I had a sudden twinge of conscience. What if there were new problem letters in the unused locker? Could I just ignore them? What if someone was really suffering and needed advice? I couldn't abandon them!

'Listen, Barbra,' I said, 'would you do me a big favour? Would you go check there's no one keeping watch on Louella's locker?'

'Yeah, sure. Why?'

'I want to make a final check for clients' letters,' I told her. 'I'll answer any letters that are already in there. Then first thing tomorrow, Louella Parsnips can pack her bags and head west, or east, or wherever the heck Honolulu is!'

'I don't think that's such a good idea,' Barbra said. 'I don't think you want to check out the locker. I really don't.'

'Why not?'

'Because!'

'Because *what*?'

'Because – because someone might see you,' Barbra said.

'Not if you stand guard for me,' I said. 'It'll only take half a minute. I'll zip in, grab any letters, and zip straight out again.'

Barbra shook her head. 'You don't want to do that,' she said. 'Trust me.'

'It'll be fine,' I assured her. 'I have to check there are no more letters. After all, if I don't pick them up, someone else might. And there are people in this school who'd really enjoy knowing other people's problems. They'd broadcast them all over! People could wind up being really embarrassed! I can't let that happen.'

She shook her head. 'Well, if you have to go to the locker, then I guess you have to,' she said. 'But it's a bad move. Don't say I didn't warn you.'

I was determined. The idea of someone like Judy MacWilliams or Maddie Fischer getting their evil claws on genuine problem letters was just too horrible! Judy is the sort of person who would broadcast the letters over the school intercom system:

'*I think everyone should know that Brandy Zeitig has an itchy rash on her backside and wants to know how to get rid of it! Hey, Brandy – have you tried changing your diaper more frequently?*'

No way! I couldn't risk something as awful as that happening.

I mean, even a totally useless advice columnist like Louella Parsnips has a responsibility to her clients.

The best way to get to Louella's locker without being spotted was to go right outside the building and approach it from the back entrance to the gym.

'Pippa?' Barbra asked as we crept across the deserted gym towards the changing rooms. 'Are you and Fern really good friends?'

I looked at her. 'Sure,' I said. It seemed an odd kind of time to ask a question like that. I mean, this was a *serious mission*.

It was as if two secret agents were sneaking into an enemy camp under the noses of armed guards, and one suddenly asks the other whether they like fried onions. Weird timing, know what I mean?

I had other things on my mind right then. Like getting to the locker without being seen, captured and totally *murdered* by a bunch of irate clients.

Barbra caught hold of my arm. 'You're

really, really good friends, huh?' she asked. 'You and Fern? And the other guys?'

'Yes. We're all really good friends. Why?'

'Oh, no reason,' Barbra said.

We crept to the doors of the locker rooms and I peered in through the glass panel.

'All clear,' I said. We pushed through the doors and made our way across the locker room floor.

'Only, I was just wondering,' Barbra said. 'Like, would Fern do anything that she knew would really upset you?'

'Of course not.'

I opened the outer door and peeped into the corridor.

'There's no one around,' I said. 'I think we're going to be OK.'

'So, if Fern wanted to, say, give you a surprise of some sort,' Barbra wittered on behind me, 'you'd take it in good heart, huh? I mean, you wouldn't be really upset?'

I looked around at her. 'Barbra, what the heck are you babbling about?'

'Nothing,' Barbra smiled. 'I was just *asking*.'

'Well, quit asking dopey questions and get out over there,' I said, pointing to the bend in the corridor. 'Keep watch, and let me know the second anyone appears, right?'

'How should I let you know?' Barbra asked.

She had a point. She could hardly yell, '*Hey, Pippa! Someone's coming!*'

'Cough,' I suggested. I demonstrated a dry, sharp cough. 'Like that. One cough if someone is heading this way; two coughs if they take off in another direction.'

'Got it.' Barbra practised a cough. She hiccuped and went into a long spasm of coughs, doubled over in the changing rooms doorway. I patted her on the back, hoping there was no one nearby. Barbra was sounding like coyotes at full moon. 'Sorry,' she spluttered, her eyes watering. 'I swallowed some spit.'

'Are you OK now?'

'Yes.'

'Good. Go keep watch.'

Barbra scuttled over to the corner and edged her head around the wall. She looked back at me and gave me the thumbs up.

I ran down past the broken drinks machine. There was Louella's locker, leaning back against the wall with its bent door. (It had been dumped back there because the lock was broken.)

I opened the door. There were three letters lying in the bottom. Three new letters. There! I'd been right to come here one final time.

I scooped the letters up and tucked them up

under my sweater. I stared down to where Barbra was standing. She was hanging halfway around the corner of the corridor. I couldn't actually *hear* anything, but I had the feeling she was talking to someone.

I tiptoed back up the corridor.

'Barbra,' I whispered, 'I'm done.'

I came up behind her and tapped her on the arm.

She nearly shot through the ceiling.

'Don't do that!' she gasped.

I peered around the corner. The corridor was empty.

'I thought you were talking to someone,' I said.

'Who?'

'How should I know who?' I said. '*Someone.*'

'Did you get the letters?' Barbra asked.

I nodded and patted the front of my sweater. 'I sure did. Three of them. Let's get out of here, before someone sees us.'

'The back way?' Barbra asked.

I nodded.

We were safe outside when a thought popped into my head.

'How did you know there would be letters?' I asked Barbra.

'I didn't.'

'So, how come you asked did I get the

letters?' I asked.

'I said, did you get *any* letters,' Barbra said.

'No, you said *the* letters.'

'Did I?' She shrugged. 'I don't remember. Hey, was that the bell for class?'

It was.

We headed inside.

Mission accomplished. I hadn't let Louella's final clients down.

As soon as I got to homeroom, I sneakily stuffed the letters right down into the very bottom of my bag. I wasn't going to risk reading them until I was safe at home.

I was a little late getting to the cafeteria at lunchtime because my favourite pen went missing. Barbra and the guys were already at our table by the time I got there. They had their heads together.

They stopped talking as I approached, and all looked around at me.

'Oh hi, Pippa,' Stacy said. 'Did you find your pen?'

I sat down. 'Yes,' I said. 'Some dumb schmuck had hidden it in the magic marker box.'

'Huh! Some people!' Cindy said. 'That's just so childish.' She smiled at me. 'We got you some food to save you lining up.'

'Thanks.'

'So,' Fern said. 'What's everyone doing after school?'

'I have to help my mom,' Stacy said.

'Me too,' Cindy said.

'Yeah,' Fern said. 'I'm going to help out in the store. I'm saving up for a ticket to San Francisco.'

Barbra's eyebrows shot up. 'San Francisco?' she said. 'Gee, how much do your folks *pay* you for helping out?'

Fern laughed. 'A measly little pittance,' she said. 'I've figured out that if I work three afternoons a week, for two hours a time, I should have enough money to buy a one-way ticket to San Francisco by the time I'm seventeen. Or by the time I'm twenty-one, if I want a round trip.'

'A person should have ambitions,' Stacy said. 'I want to learn to pilot a helicopter, so I can fly over those huge African wildlife reserves and make movies of herds of rhino and wildebeest and – hey! Watch out, you big elephant!' She was interrupted by Simon Lundy, who came barging past our table with a face like Droopy the dog on a bad hair day. He nearly knocked Stacy right off her chair.

'You shouldn't get in the way,' he snarled. He was in one awful mood.

'I was sitting down eating my lunch!' Stacy yelled. 'How come I got in *your* way?'

'What's the problem, Simon?' Fern asked.

'I was dumb enough to write Louella Parsnips for some advice,' Simon growled.

I noticed that a few heads turned and a good few ears pricked up in interest. Simon was the first person to have actually owned up to sending Louella a letter. Everyone else was hanging on his words, waiting to see what had happened.

'So?' Fern said impatiently. 'Cough it up. What's the problem?'

Simon told them the story of the accidental phone call to Dubai.

'And that half-witted so-called advice columnist told me to confess and to offer to pay the money back out of my allowance,' Simon raved. 'She said that if I *offered*, then my dad would let me off 'cos he'd be so pleased that I was acting responsibly. The stupid idiot!'

'Your dad?' Barbra asked.

'No! Louella Parsnips!' Simon hollered.

'Why? What happened?' I asked.

'What happened?' Simon gibbered. 'I'll tell you what happened! My dad agreed with me, that's what happened! He's going to take back half my allowance until the bill is paid! And he wouldn't even have thought of it if I hadn't said anything. And it's all that dingbat Louella Parsnips' fault!'

'We should do something about her!' Sophie Carpenter called from a nearby table. 'She's a total menace!'

'I agree,' shouted Denise DiNovi. 'We should make her keep her stupid advice to herself!'

'We should make her eat those useless letters!' Amanda Allen yelled across the cafeteria. 'She doesn't know *anything*!' (I'd figured that the 'A.' who had written complaining about her pesky little sister was Amanda – Stacy's big sister. I'd written back that everyone was entitled to a fair use of the phone and that people should learn to share and share alike. I guess that advice hadn't gone down too well.)

Anyhow, Amanda had a lot of support for her idea that Louella should eat her own letters. It seemed like Louella Parsnips had suddenly become public enemy number one.

The rest of that lunch break turned into an impromptu meeting of the Louella Parsnips Loathe-Club.

You can bet I kept really, *really* quiet.

'Well,' Fern said, smiling at me. 'I'm sure glad *I'm* not Louella Parsnips.'

'Yeah,' I said with a sickly grin. 'Me too.'

'Do you want to come back to my house?' Barbra asked me after school had finished.

'I want to,' I said. 'But I have some work to do.' I leaned close to her so no one else could overhear. 'The letters,' I hissed in her ear.

'You're not still going to reply to them, are you?' Barbra asked. 'Why bother? You heard what everyone thinks of Louella.'

'I think I should read them at least,' I said. 'There might be one person in this school who could use a little help.'

Barbra grinned. 'Yeah,' she laughed. 'You!'

'I don't know how stuff goes *so* wrong,' I mumbled. 'I really don't!'

'Look, I'll tell you what,' Barbra said. 'Why not come back to my house and we'll read the letters together?'

'Shhh!' I hissed. People were walking past. I didn't want my cover blown. I didn't want to be torn to shreds by an angry mob in front of my own school.

On the other hand, having Barbra read the last three letters with me might be a really good idea. Maybe *her* advice wouldn't turn out to be such a disaster.

I took Barbra up on her offer. After all, what did I have to lose? The chances were that the letters were from people telling Louella what an idiot she was anyway.

Mrs Plum was busy with something in the living room, so we just grabbed a sandwich and a can of soda each and went into Barbra's bedroom.

'OK,' I said, hauling the three envelopes out of my bag. 'Here goes nothing!' I dropped the letters on the bed. I looked at Barbra. She was checking her watch – for the tenth time since we'd arrived.

'Why are you so interested in the time?' I asked.

'I'm not,' Barbra said. 'I don't want to miss *Spindrift*.'

'*Spindrift* isn't on for another hour and a half,' I said.

'Oh, yeah. Of course.' Barbra sat on the bed opposite me. 'Well?' she said. 'Are you going to open them?'

I picked one up.

Dear Louella,

My problem is that I have a friend with some really bad habits. She is my best friend, really, but she grosses me out sometimes with the way she makes these awful noises when she eats. And she walks around all afternoon with food stuck between her teeth. And she smells funny. I don't want to hurt her feelings, but I think she needs to know what a total slob she is. What can I do to make her less of a social embarrassment?

Thanks in advance for any help you can give me,

Yours,

Fern Kipsak

‘Aaaargggghhhh!’

I stared at the letter. I couldn’t believe my eyes. Fern was my best friend. I was her best friend. The letter was about me! Fern thought I was a slob and a social embarrassment. I was *devastated*!

‘Pippa?’ Barbra asked in surprise at my sudden ‘Aaaargggghhhh!’ ‘What’s the matter? What’s in the letter?’

‘Ugh, oog, gruggg,’ I gurgled, staring from Barbra to the letter. ‘Noth-nuth-nith-*nothing*!’ I managed to say.

‘There must be *something* in it,’ Barbra said. ‘Show me.’ She reached over for it.

I scrunched the letter up and stuffed it into my pocket.

‘It’s boring,’ I said. ‘Not worth worrying about. Let’s try the next one.’

She shrugged and handed me the next letter.

Fern’s letter had made me feel quite queasy in my stomach. I mean, it isn’t every day that you find out what your so-called best friend in all the world *really* thinks of you. Sheesh – how was I going to face Fern tomorrow without just curling up and dying of embarrassment? I felt totally, utterly and completely *awful*! I didn't want Barbra to know how upset I was. I had to stop myself from collapsing on the bed and just *howling*! How could Fern *think* stuff like that about me?

The front doorbell rang.

'I'll just go see who that is,' Barbra said, leaping off the bed like a jack-in-the-box. She closed the bedroom door behind her.

Meanwhile, I opened the next letter. Maybe it would take my mind off that dreadfull letter from Fern.

Dear Louella Parsnips,

I have a really terrible problem. Last week I received a letter from a lawyer in New York who gave me some awful and totally unbelievable news. He has absolute proof that my mom and dad are not my real mom and dad at all. He has a letter from a nurse who worked in the hospital where I was born. In the letter she admits that there was an awful MIX-UP! I was mixed up with another baby who was born at the same time, and we ended up with the WRONG

PARENTS! He also has a copy of my real birth certificate. My real mother is called Cleopatra Peabody, and she is a CIA operative who works in Bulgaria, and my dad is ACE HAWKMAN, lead singer with the Black Hawks rock band. Of course, my mom and dad don't KNOW this. I do not know what to do! Should I TELL them and risk breaking their hearts, or should I say nothing about it and GO INSANE because of keeping such a huge secret? A quick reply would be appreciated.

Yours,

Stacy Allen

I was still sitting there staring at the letter with my eyes bugging and my jaw hanging open when Barbra came back into the room.

'Well?' she said. 'What's in it?'

I handed her the letter.

She sat down and read it.

'Whoo!' she breathed. 'Poor Stacy. That's just awful.'

'I'll say,' I croaked.

'I mean, imagine finding out that Ace Hawkman was your dad,' Barbra added. 'The Black Hawks are terrible!! My mom has a couple of albums by them. Yuck!'

I stared at her. 'Never mind *that*!' I howled.

'You *would* mind if you had to listen to the

albums,' Barbra said. 'They're useless to the max!'

'I think you're kind of missing the point,' I said to Barbra as calmly as I could. 'Stacy's folks *aren't* her folks! She's asking Louella what she should do.' I grabbed her arm. 'What do we tell her?'

'Hmm,' Barbra said. 'Tricky.'

She sounded like she had been asked to decide between pistachio- or strawberry-flavoured ice cream. And at the same time, my brain was going into a major meltdown!

'How about reading the last letter while we think about it?' Barbra said.

'Guuh?'

She pointed at the final envelope.

I picked it up. I had a really uneasy feeling about it. What would it be? *I have discovered that Fern Kipsak is an alien from another planet?* (After all, Fern was always blathering on about aliens). Or possibly: *We have discovered that you are really Pippa Kane. We will call at your house tonight to hack you into tiny pieces with a small but very sharp fruit knife. Signed, the whole of your class.*

Dear Louella,

I overheard a conversation yesterday between the School Principal and a man who looked like a gangster. The gangster guy gave the Principal a whole lot of money. The Principal said he would turn a blind eye when the gangster robbed the school. What is a blind eye? I think the Principal can see just fine. I think the gangster is going to steal all our electrical and computer equipment. No one will believe me. What do you advise me to do?

Desperately worried.

PS The gangster is going to rob our school on Wednesday night.

'So?' Barbra said. 'What's it say?'

'Uh, oh, nothing much,' I mumbled. 'Would it be OK for me to go hide in your closet for a week or two? I won't be a nuisance. Promise.'

Barbra plucked the letter out of my hand.

She let out a long, low whistle. 'Whoooo-eeee-ooooo.'

Have you seen those cartoons where steam comes out of someone's ears and the top of their head blows off? Yeah, you know what I'm talking about. Well, meet Pippa, the living, ear-steaming, wig-flipping brain-exploding cartoon character!

Barbra looked at me. 'Are you OK? You look a little pale.'

'I'm fine,' I breathed. 'I'm just fine. I'm totally fine. No problem. Heh, heh, heh.' I stared at her. 'I'm thinking of maybe leaving town. I hear Rio de Janeiro is really nice this time of year.'

'That's OK, then,' Barbra said. 'If you're fine. Uh, I'm kind of peckish. Shall I get us a pack of tortilla chips?'

Was she kidding me, or what?

'Barbra?' I asked. 'What are we gonna do about these letters?'

She smiled. 'I have an idea. It's a little off the wall, OK? You might not go for it, but it's a real old tradition in our family, and it *always* works.'

I stared at her. What on earth was she talking about? An old family tradition?

'Do you want me to set it up?' she asked brightly. 'It'll only take a couple of minutes.'

'Sure,' I murmured. 'What *exactly* is this old family tradition?'

Barbra smiled. 'You'll see,' she said. She got up off the bed. 'It's a little strange until you get used to it, but it isn't dangerous at all.'

It isn't *dangerous*? At *all*?

She walked over to the window and pulled down the blind. The room got really dark. Next she took a flashlight out of a drawer and switched it on.

'Candles would be better,' she said cheerfully. 'But this should work OK.'

She went over to her closet and rummaged around in the bottom.

'Barbra,' I said, 'what did you mean when you said it wasn't *dangerous*?'

She looked around at me. 'Exactly that.'

'Yeah, but people don't say stuff isn't dangerous unless they're talking about something that seems like it might be dangerous. See what I mean?'

'Aha!' Barbra exclaimed, ignoring my question. 'Here we are!'

She stood up and turned around. Between her hands she was holding a glass globe. She came over to the bed and carefully sat the ball of glass down in front of me.

'What's that?' I asked.

'It's our crystal ball,' Barbra said. She sat cross-legged opposite me and jammed the flashlight down between her legs so it shone up into her face. She suddenly looked weird and creepy. 'It's been in our family for seven generations,' she said. 'We use it to call up my great-great-great-great-aunts.' She looked at me, her face all screwy with strange-shaped shadows thrown up by the flashlight. 'My family always calls up Aunt Florence and Aunt Clemence and Aunt Lavinia when we have problems.'

'... call ... up ...?' I said. 'Uh, what exactly do you mean by *call up*?' I stared at the crystal ball, glowing away in its nest of bedcovers.

'Call up their *spirits*, of course, silly!' Barbra said. 'They've been dead for years and years and years. Here's what we do: I'll call them up for you, and then you can ask them what you should do about the problems. They'll come up with some great answers, honest. They always do.'

I looked uneasily at Barbra. Was this a put-on? Was she kidding me? Or – gulp! – did she really think she could use that glass ball to chat with the spirits of her dead aunts?

'Um, actually,' I began, 'I think I'd better be getting home soon. Maybe we could do this another time, huh?'

Barbra closed her eyes and began to moan. 'Ooooogh. Mooooogh. Woooogh. Groooogh.'

I felt the shivers creeping up my spine.

'Barbra?' I said quietly. 'Do you have a pain?'

'I call on the spirits of the three wise aunts!' Barbra's sudden shout nearly startled me out of my wits. 'Are you there, Aunt Lavinia? Are you there, Aunt Clemence? Are you there, Aunt Florence?'

That was it! The girl was insane! I was out of there!

'Knock to show you hear me!' Barbra yelled.

I lifted myself off the bed and began to tiptoe towards the door.

'Knock three times if you are there!' Barbra howled.

Knock!

I stopped like I'd hit a wall. Someone – or some*thing* – had knocked heavily on Barbra's bedroom door.

Knock! Knock!

Two more knocks sounded on the door.

That was three knocks in all! Three knocks! One knock for each of Barbra's great-great-great-great-aunts.

'Enter!' Barbra bellowed. 'Enter and give your all-seeing advice to my friend Pippa!'

Yikes! The door began to open.

I back-pedalled. The hallway outside was in darkness. Three shapeless things were standing in the doorway.

The things came towards me.

I let out a shriek as the three shapes jumped all over me. Something was thrown over my head and I was squished down into the carpet.

I writhed about, shrieking on the floor with Barbra's three dead aunts climbing all over me. If I hadn't been so busy struggling to get out from under the thing that they'd thrown over me, I guess my entire life would have flashed before my eyes.

It didn't.

I heard giggles. The giggles turned to chuckles. Then the chuckles turned into full-scale howls of laughter.

I struggled out from under the thing – which turned out to be a sheet. Fern and Stacy and Cindy were rolling around on the carpet, yelling with laughter.

Barbra was laughing, too. She climbed off the bed and switched on the main light.

'You . . . you . . . you *rats*!' I shouted. 'You could have *killed* me! I nearly died of fright!'

Fern sat up, wiping her eyes. 'Serves you right!' she said. 'Louella Parsnips!'

I glared at Barbra. 'You told them! You told them, after you promised you wouldn't!'

She shook her head. 'No, they told me,' she said. 'I already knew you were Louella Parsnips before you confessed it to me.'

I was stunned. 'They did?' I looked at them. 'You did?'

Stacy nodded. 'It wasn't too difficult to figure out,' she said. 'I got suspicious when you said you couldn't come to the mall on Sunday because of English homework. We didn't have any English homework.'

'So we figured out you had to be doing something else,' Cindy said. 'Something you didn't want us to know about.'

'Like answering Louella's mail,' Fern said. 'And then there was that little incident in math class, when Denise called Mr Tove, Mr Toad.' She pointed to herself. 'I was the one who said Mr Townes looked like a toad and you borrowed the idea!'

'That's right,' Stacy said. 'And you were dumb enough to ask us about people having crushes on teachers. Like we wouldn't be able to put two and two together, Pippa!'

'So, you've known all along!' I gasped. 'Right from the start!'

'No, not right from the start,' Stacy said. 'But we had it figured out a couple of days ago.'

I stared at Fern. 'So why did you go along with the puppy idea, if you knew I was Louella?'

Fern shrugged. 'It sounded like it might work,' she said. 'I should have known something would go wrong!'

'Does everyone know about me being Louella?' I asked miserably.

'Not yet,' Cindy said. 'Not unless we tell them.'

That was when the final piece clicked into place. 'The letters were all made up!' I gasped. 'That stuff about the Principal and the gangster.'

'I thought that one up,' Cindy said.

'Did you really believe Ace Hawkman could *possibly* be my dad?' Stacy said.

'No!' I said, lying through my teeth. 'Not for a second. How dumb do you think I am? And you don't have to answer that, Fern!'

'We thought you needed teaching a lesson,' Stacy said. 'So we fixed this whole thing up with Barbra. The letters and the spooky aunts and everything.'

'The spook-stuff was my idea,' Fern said with a grin. 'Neat, huh?'

Barbra looked at me. 'I warned you not to go to the locker,' she said. 'I said you wouldn't like it.'

No wonder Barbra had been behaving in a strange way earlier on in school. She'd tried to warn me off. And that was why she had asked me whether Fern was a real good friend. She knew what Fern had planned for me!

'I wouldn't have gone along with it if you hadn't told me that Fern would never do anything to really upset you,' Barbra said. 'She said you'd be mad at first, but that you'd see the funny side.' She looked at me. 'You do see the funny side, don't you?'

I blinked around at them. 'I guess so,' I said. Did I?

'I had you completely fooled about the talent contest in Mayfield, didn't I?' Cindy said. 'You really believed my mom had put me in for it.'

I nodded. 'You should audition for *Spindrift*, Cindy,' I said. 'That was some performance!'

'The fact is,' said Cindy. 'Devon Palminieri never even *came* to my house to practise the clarinet. She practises at *school* these days, so she didn't need somewhere quiet! I just figured out what *might* have happened if I *had* taken your advice.' She grinned. 'You can't be mad at us. You *did* need teaching a lesson.'

'You just can't go around giving people advice,' Stacy added. 'It's not what you're good at, Pippa.'

I sighed. 'So, what am I good at? Apart from

acting like a total idiot.'

Fern grinned at me. 'You're good at plenty of things,' she said. 'You're clever and brainy and funny and kooky and a total weirdo. That's why you're my best friend.'

I looked at her. 'Even though I eat like a pig and smell terrible?'

Fern laughed. 'Yeah, even though you eat like a pig and smell terrible!'

'Well, *thanks*, Fern! That's real big of you.'

'My pleasure.'

I looked anxiously at her. 'You were kidding in that letter, right?'

She grinned. 'Of course I was!'

'So? Are you going to quit the advice business?' Cindy asked.

'You bet I am!' I put my face in my hands. 'I wish I'd never started,' I moaned. 'Are you guys going to tell everyone?'

'Not if you agree to do exactly what we say,' Fern said.

I peered at her from between my fingers. 'Which is?'

'Well, for a start, you can shut up shop as Louella Parsnips,' Stacy said.

'I was going to anyway,' I said. 'I was going to put up a notice saying she had to leave on account of stress and overwork and stuff.'

'Not good enough,' Stacy said. 'Barbra? Do

you have that resignation letter we worked out?'

'Sure.' Barbra dug a sheet of paper out of her bag and handed it to me.

'We want you to type this up on your mom's computer and pin it on the notice board first thing tomorrow,' Cindy said.

I read the resignation letter.

Dear Everyone,

I am afraid I will not be able to help you out with your problems any more. I have recently discovered that I am totally unsuited to a life as an advice columnist. I am probably the worst problem solver in the country. In fact, I am an idiot! A total idiot! I would like to apologise to all those who took my advice. I plan on moving immediately to a wooden shack in the middle of nowhere and spending the rest of my life as a hermit. Goodbye, and sorry about all the bad advice.

Yours,

Louella Parsnips

I nodded. I could deal with that.

'Is that all I have to do?' I asked.

'You're kidding?' Fern said. 'That's just for starters!'

'What else?' I asked.

'We haven't decided yet,' Stacy said. 'The jury's still out on that.'

'Don't worry, Pippa,' Cindy said. 'We'll think of something!'

Yes. I kind of thought they would!

Mrs Plum popped her head around the door. 'Hello, you guys,' she said with a smile. 'Are you having fun?'

'We sure are,' Barbra said.

'I've got something to show you.' Mrs Plum came into the room. She held up a knitted sweater. 'Fresh off the knitting needles!' she said with a grin. 'What do you think?'

It was a short-sleeved orange top with a really neat, super-cool cartoon cat in shades on the front.

'Mom, it's wonderful!' Barbra exploded. 'I want to try it! I want to try it!'

Ten seconds later and Barbra was in her new top and admiring herself in the mirror on her closet door.

Mrs Plum looked absolutely delighted.

'Barbra chose the pattern herself,' she said. 'We took a trip down to the mall and she picked out a bunch of designs for me to knit up for her.' She smiled. 'It makes a whole lot more sense than me choosing patterns that she doesn't like.'

'That's great!' Stacy said. 'Could you knit some stuff for me, Mrs Plum? If I supply the wool?'

'I don't see why not,' Mrs Plum said.

'And me!' Cindy piped up.

In the end we all wanted Mrs Plum to knit stuff for us.

'OK! OK! Enough!' Mrs Plum said with a laugh. 'I only have one pair of hands. But I'll see what I can do.'

'Come and look at the other patterns I picked out, guys,' Barbra said.

'You do that,' Mrs Plum said. 'And while you're looking, how about I go slice up an Alabama fudge cake that I just happen to have?'

Everyone thought that was a great idea.

We headed into the living room.

Barbra caught hold of my arm and stopped me while the others went through.

'I hope you're not mad at me for setting you up with Fern and the others,' she said.

I shook my head. 'I guess it was kind of dumb of me to think I could give people good advice.'

'You helped me a whole lot, you know,' Barbra said. 'If you hadn't made me realise I needed to *talk* with my mom, we would never have had the idea of going to the mall together and picking out patterns I actually liked.'

I smiled. 'So, I guess my advice isn't always terrible.'

'It wasn't *advice*, Pippa,' Barbra reminded me. 'That was the whole point, remember?'

'Oh, yeah. That's right.'

'Thanks all the same,' Barbra said. 'You're a real pal.'

'Hey, Pippa,' Fern called from the living room. 'Get a load of these really cool clothes!'

The guys were sitting around the coffee table. A lot of sweater designs were spread out on the table top. Barbra and I kneeled down with them and we all went through the designs, trying to decide which we liked best.

Stacy shook her head. 'I'm useless at choosing clothes,' she said. 'I'm going to need some advice on what looks best on me.'

For some reason, everyone looked at me.

I shrugged. 'Don't ask me,' I said. 'I'm out of the advice business. Permanently!'

Everyone thought that was really funny. I even laughed myself, to be honest.

I guess I'll just have to get used to going through my entire life as Pippa the Jinx! Sigh! All those wasted great ideas – and all because of some dumb jinx! A person could get really fed up!

'Alabama fudge cake!' Mrs Plum called. She came in carrying a loaded tray.

I picked a slice of the gooey, sticky cake and took a mega-huge bite. It tasted utterly wonderful.

Hey, maybe life wasn't so very bad after all.

I thought that, like, two *seconds* before a big splob of my caramel sauce somehow went *spludge* all over Cindy's sleeve.

'Pippa!' Cindy yelled. 'For heaven's sake! Watch out!'

Fern nearly choked herself trying not to laugh.

'You'd better get a cloth, Pippa,' Mrs Plum said.

Barbra looked sympathetically at me, but Stacy just shook her head as if I was a hopeless case.

Maybe she was right.

Maybe I should wear a sign saying *Beware of the Pippa*.

This is Pippa the Jinx signing off in order to go fetch a cloth from the Plums' kitchen.

Can't wait to find out what the girls get up to next? Well, worry not. Check out Chapter One from the next fabulous 'Stacy and Friends' book:

My Sister, My Slave

'My arm's getting stiff,' I told Amanda. 'Is there any chance of you finishing off in the next three months?'

I must have been lying there holding that apple for half the afternoon. I mean, I don't mind helping my sister out with her art projects, but there are limits to how long a person wants to sit clutching an apple and not daring to move while a person's older sister is drawing her.

'Five minutes, Stacy, and I'll be through,' Amanda said.

'You said that ten minutes ago,' I reminded her.

'You can't rush art,' Amanda said.

'You could kind of *nudge* it along though, couldn't you?' I said.

I'd only volunteered to be Amanda's sitter because Mom was having one of her crazy cleaning days down in the kitchen. Posing for Amanda was a good way of getting out of being hauled off down there to help.

There were plenty of other things I could have been doing. For starters, I was a whole week behind in my diary entries. I could imagine today's entry: *Sunday. Broke the all-America apple-holding record, junior division.*

'I can't concentrate if you keep talking,' Amanda said, frowning at me over the drawing board she had propped up on her knees.

I sighed and wriggled myself into a more comfortable position on her bed.

'Don't move!' Amanda snapped. Amanda likes to snap. Maybe Mom watched a lot of programmes about alligators while she was carrying Amanda.

My sister says it's actually because she has an *artistic temperament.*

The Stacy Allen Dictionary
Artistic Temperament: A real good way for some people to get away with being snappy and bad-tempered.

'You're only drawing my *hand*,' I said. 'How long can that take?'

'I want to do it right,' Amanda said. 'It's very distracting the way you keep squirming around.'

'Sorr-ee,' I said. 'It's not like I'm getting paid for this, you know. Some people might be grateful. Some people might think some kind of reward was called for.'

'No problem,' Amanda said. 'You get to eat the apple when I'm through, OK?'

'You're all heart,' I said. 'Did you know you wiggle your toes when you're drawing?'

You get to notice things like that when you've got nothing to do but stare into space for an hour.

I guess I should explain my sister a bit. She's thirteen. I'm ten, by the way, but she isn't three years older than me. It just looks that way right now because it was her thirteenth birthday recently and my eleventh birthday doesn't come for another five months. After that, she'll only be two years older than me. If you see what I mean.

You wouldn't think we were sisters, though, if you saw us walking down the street together. I take after my dad whereas Amanda's inherited her wavy blonde hair and her big blue eyes from Mom. What have I inherited? Crooked teeth and light brown hair that's so straight you'd think I went over it with an iron every morning before I hit the streets. Oh, yeah, I've inherited some real amusing freckles, too, and the kind of shape that you usually see in a *field* scaring crows off the crops.

I'd give you a big smile, but right now the brace on my teeth might dazzle you. I've got to wear it for two *years*!

It's a little too early to tell what my baby brother Sam's inherited from Mom and Dad. He's only thirteen months old. I've got big plans for Sam. I'm going to teach him everything I know. He's the sweetest baby in the whole wide world, and I'm going to be the best sister a kid brother could ever wish for.

Where was I? Oh, yes, explaining Amanda.

Easy, Step by Step Recipe for Making Your Own Amanda Allen

1. Take one cheerleader's outfit and place in a bowl.
2. Stir in some blonde hair, blue eyes, and a figure that's starting to get kind of curvy here and there. (But not as curvy as she'd like it to be.)
3. Add a whole bunch of dumb ideas about boys and trendy clothes.
4. Mix in three air-head friends called Cheryl, Rachel and Natalie.
5. Add a telephone to help with the hectic social life. (The entire recipe falls apart without a telephone.)
6. Season with a sprinkle or two of Genuine Artistic Ability.

7. Add a real superior attitude and mix well.
8. Place mixture in a house in Four Corners, Indiana.
Thirteen years later you'll have one Amanda Allen, AKA Bimbo Surprise!